STARGATE
ATLÅNTIS™

LOST QUEEN

MELISSA SCOTT

FANDEMONIUM BOOKS

An original publication of Fandemonium Ltd, produced under license from MGM Consumer Products.

Fandemonium Books
United Kingdom
Visit our website: www.stargatenovels.com

STARGATE
ATLÅNTIS
™

METRO-GOLDWYN-MAYER Presents
STARGATE ATLANTIS™
JOE FLANIGAN RACHEL LUTTRELL JASON MOMOA JEWEL STAITE
ROBERT PICARDO and DAVID HEWLETT as Dr. McKay
Executive Producers BRAD WRIGHT & ROBERT C. COOPER
Created by BRAD WRIGHT & ROBERT C. COOPER

WWW.MGM.COM

Print ISBN: 978-1-905586-74-5 Ebook ISBN: 978-1-80070-060-4

CAST OF CHARACTERS

<u>Appearing in the story:</u>

Blaze — Consort to the Queen Moonwhite

Distant Thunder — Master of Sciences Physical to Queen Light Breaking

Everlasting — Consort to the Queen Light Breaking

Forge — Master of Sciences Biological to the Queen Light Breaking

Guide — Wraith nicknamed "Todd" by the Atlantis Expedition, currently their uneasy ally; father of Queen Alabaster and currently her valued advisor

Icewind — Master of Sciences Physical to the Queen Moonwhite

Light Breaking — Wraith Queen; daughter of Edge and sister of Moonwhite

Moonwhite — Wraith Queen; daughter of Edge and sister of Light Breaking

Red Moon — blade and Dart pilot, member of Queen Moonwhite's hive

Rising Tide — Master of Sciences Biological to Queen Moonwhite

Salt — storymaker; formerly of Edge's zenana and now advisor to both Light Breaking and Moonwhite

Whisper — blade and pilot, member of Queen Moonwhite's hive

<u>Mentioned but not appearing:</u>

Alabaster — young Wraith Queen, daughter of Guide; currently in an uneasy alliance with the Atlantis

Expedition that involves allowing Dr. Jennifer Keller to do research among her people.

Cloud — one of the nine First Mothers, founders of the Wraith

Death — Wraith Queen, now dead, who attempted to bring all the Wraith hives under her control by eliminating other Queens

Deep Water — Wraith Queen defeated by Edge, now dead

Dustwind — Master of Sciences Physical to Queen Edge, now dead

Edge — Wraith Queen, mother of Light Breaking and Moonwhite, now dead

Ember — Master of Sciences Biological to the Queen Alabaster, working with Jennifer Keller on a retrovirus that would allow humans to survive being fed on by a Wraith

Gryphon — one of the nine First Mothers, founders of the Wraith

Jewelbright — Master of Sciences Biological to Queen Edge, now dead

Night — one of the nine First Mothers, founders of the Wraith

Osprey — one of the nine First Mothers, founders of the Wraith

Sky — one of the nine First Mothers, founders of the Wraith

Steelflower — Wraith Queen impersonated by Teyla Emmagen with Guide's assistance

A note on Wraith names: the Wraith are a telepathic

species, and do not seem to give each other "names" in the sense of individual identifiers as humans do. Instead, they appear to recognize each other by the mental "tone," the image produced by another Wraith's habit of mind, and among themselves refer to each other by that image. The names in the text are rough translations of those images.

Glossary

Terms Used Among the Wraith

Blade — a warrior, usually attached to a particular hive and its Queen

Cleverman — a scientist, usually attached to a particular hive and its Queen

Commander — the captain, usually a blade, of any ship smaller than a hiveship

Consort — a Queen's acknowledged partner and usually the leader of the hive's blades

Dart — fast, single-seat spaceship often used for culling

Drone — a soldier; drones are bred quickly and without mental autonomy, and are usually under the direct control of a Queen, blade, or cleverman

Hivemaster — the commander of a hiveship and the person responsible for its maintenance and upkeep, as well as for the care of the drones; his job makes him a member of the Queen's zenana

Kine — Wraith collective term for humans

Master of Sciences Biological — one of two chief scientists of a hive, in charge of all biological research and all clevermen specializing in biology

Master of Sciences Physical — one of two chief scientists of a hive, in charge of all non-biological research and all clevermen not specializing in biology

Pallax — a blade or cleverman who enjoys the queen's favor

Storymaker — a Wraith male who functions as an entertainer for a hive, creating illusions that tell a story; storymakers are considered neither blades nor clevermen, but stand outside that system

Zenana — a Queen's council, made up of the hive's officers, her Consort (if any), and her favorites among the crew; also, by extension, the compartment of the hive in which the zenana meets

Orthographic note: telepathic communication between Wraith is indicated by *asterisks*

CHAPTER ONE

FORGE had spent nearly a ten-day in Alabaster's hive, consulting with her Master of Sciences Biological nearly every waking moment, and the weight of everything he had learned lay heavy on him. Perhaps these new ideas would work; more likely they would not, or not the way Alabaster's man thought, but his own queen had been right, they were worth considering at least a little further. That was what he would tell her, along with all the details, but at the moment what he wanted, even more than her regard and praise, was to sleep and to feed. Or perhaps it should be in the opposite order; he closed his eyes for an instant, his hand-mouth throbbing, and imagined the sweet flow of life restoring him. He had not fed on Alabaster's hive, an old-fashioned point of etiquette, but one that his own queen would approve. One did not share the contents of the feeding pens with any but close allies, and in this case in particular, where some of the humans were willing donors, he thought she was right to insist.

A tone sounded, and he straightened, seeing his own hive loom out of the night, a shadow against the stars. He reached for the comm controls, but before he could send the recognition signal, a voice spoke from the speakers.

"Forge. Bring your scout alongside at once. The Queen requires your presence."

Forge recognized the voice instantly: Everlasting, the Queen's Consort and the nearest thing he had to a friend in the zenana, the queen's favorites who managed the hive under her authority. "Very well," he said, though had they been speaking mind-to-mind rather than over the comm system he would have been hard pressed to hide his annoyance.

He slid the scout neatly into its dock in the hive's underbelly, deliberately waiting until all the redundant checks showed clear before he opened the hatch. Everlasting was waiting there, tall and hard-faced, his hair shaven to reveal a complex tattoo that covered his scalp and left cheek with coiling lines: the style of the blades of Sky's lineage, and an unmistakable reminder that the Queen favored him. Forge straightened, aware that his own hair was in disarray and that he had been wearing the same plain coat for the entire trip, and did his best to pretend it didn't matter.

I am here. Unwashed and unfed, but if the Queen wants me now...

He let the thought trail off, hoping it would be enough of a hint, but Everlasting ignored the suggestion. *Come.*

For a moment, Forge considered a more open protest, but Everlasting's mind was closed tight, not even the faintest taste of his feelings leaking out at the edges. And that was unusual — Everlasting was rarely anything less than open, a mind determinedly straightforward — enough so that Forge followed without complaint as the Consort led him through the hive to the zenana. The drones at the door moved aside for them, and the door itself slid back to reveal a room nearly empty, only the Queen herself, Light Breaking, standing with one hand on the back of her throne. Beyond her, Forge saw the old storymaker Salt, who had served Light Breaking's mother and now divided his time between the hives of the two daughters. Both things were unexpected enough that he stopped short, the door sliding closed behind him.

We are here, Everlasting said, and Forge caught a distinct sense of relief from Salt before Light Breaking whirled on them. She was a daughter of Night's lineage, tall and full-breasted, her jet-black hair caught in a web of silver wires that pulled it up and back to spill behind her like the currents on a dark river. Her gold eyes fixed on him, and Forge went to one knee, feeling her anger and, beneath it, fear. It was only then that he saw the lit screen, and the face within it: Blaze, the Consort of Light Breaking's sister Moonwhite.

"And not before time." Light Breaking bared teeth in a snarl, then tuned back to face the screen. "Now. You may speak, since I have witnesses to what you say."

"Lady." Blaze took a careful breath. He was a blade of Cloud, not of Night, one of the young men who had come courting the two queens, earning places in their hives and eventually in their favor. Forge had been one such himself, a cleverman of Gryphon come to a hive of Night with only his skills to recommend him, and he knew how precarious Blaze's place could be. "I am come to you because my Queen, Moonwhite, left fifty hours ago to visit you, and she has not returned. We have sought her on the most likely return course, but now we begin to fear she never reached you."

Very diplomatic. Forge grimaced, not having meant to let that thought escape him, despite its being true enough. The two sisters had been enough at odds over this plan of Alabaster's that one might expect violence between them. Light Breaking shot him a glance, silent disapproval, and Everlasting shook his head.

"She never reached us —"

Light Breaking lifted her hand. "Silence. You did not know." She looked at the screen. "My sister was here, and we spoke as she wished — in private, which is why you, my lords, have heard nothing of it until now. But she left us twenty-three — no, twenty-five hours ago, now. I fear that you are right, something has gone terribly wrong."

There was silence from the screen, Blaze's eyebrow ridges rising for an instant before he controlled his expression. "She has been, and left. And you were not concerned?"

Forge caught his breath at the open challenge, and Everlasting bared his teeth, but Light Breaking merely shook her head. "Why should I be? She had the answer she wanted, and all was well. It was not a long or diffi-cult journey back to you."

"And yet," Blaze said. "She is not here."

"And now I am concerned," Light Breaking said. "What help can I give you? Ask, and you shall have."

Blaze dipped his head again. "My hope is that her scout had some internal trouble that forced her to set down on an intermediate world. I have sent Darts back along the most likely flight path, but if you would do the same, we could cover the ground much more efficiently."

"Done." Light Breaking looked over her shoulder, nodding to Everlasting. "My Consort will see to that."

"Thank you," Blaze said. "And of course if you have any idea of her planned course, or even her departure heading, that would be helpful."

"For the latter, I will inquire of the Hivemaster," Light Breaking said. "My understanding was that she planned to take the swiftest course. She did not want to be too long gone from her hive."

"Thank you," Blaze said again, and for the first time looked past her to Everlasting. "My Darts have begun combing the systems nearest us. If you could do the same —"

"I leave that to you and Everlasting to decide," Light Breaking said sharply. "Consort, take up this conversation elsewhere — and bring in the Hivemaster, he may well have seen something useful. But for now — leave me."

"I will contact you directly," Everlasting said, to Blaze. Blaze nodded and the queen broke the connection. Everlasting bowed to her and backed toward the doors. Forge turned to follow, but Light Breaking lifted her hand.

Not you. I want to know what you found on Alabaster's hive.

Forge bowed to hide his surprise. *As you wish, Lady.*

You'll stay, too, Light Breaking said, to Salt, and settled herself comfortably on her throne, the bleached bone curving to cradle her. *Now. Tell me about this retrovirus. Will it work?*

Forge took a deep breath, trying to shake his own thoughts back into order. Surely her missing sister was of more importance than Alabaster's dealings with the Lanteans — but then, it was rare enough for queens to acknowledge their biological sisters, never mind work in tandem as these two had. Only their cooperation had kept both hives clear of Queen Death's disastrous war. And that was not a thought he wanted to allow near the surface of his mind. *It seems to have worked so far,* he said cautiously. *Alabaster's Master of Sciences Biological showed me his work, and the work of the Lantean female who has been working with them, and I could find no flaws. He and his men said they had fed on humans who had taken the treatment, and neither they nor the humans had taken any harm.*

Not like Hoff, Light Breaking said, with a dark smile.

Not at all. Forge suppressed a shudder. The Hoffans had poisoned themselves — infected themselves with a virus that had killed half their own population in exchange for poisoning any Wraith who fed upon them.

Did you test it yourself?

Forge shook his head. *I did not, though I would not hesitate to do so another time. But I thought that feeding from their cells was more of a commitment than I should make.*

I agree with that, Salt said.

A wise decision. Light Breaking leaned back in her throne. *And what are they offering to persuade us to try this great experiment of theirs?*

Nothing directly, Forge answered. *At least not so far. There was no mention, for example, of any alliance, though I would not rule out the possibility. And they have good relations with the Lanteans, which could stand us in good stead.*

Salt cocked his head to one side. He was of an older generation, his skin faded and his hair thinning, so that he wore it pulled back into a single narrow braid. *You distrust them.*

Forge glanced at him, and then at the queen. When she said nothing, he said, *I trust the work. I believe that this retrovirus will do everything that Ember says, and the Fair One, the human cleverman —*

Light Breaking spoke her name aloud. "Jennifer Keller."

Yes. Forge dipped his head. *Her work is robust.*

How many times can a human be fed upon, and how often? Light Breaking asked.

That has not yet been determined, Forge answered. *With the Fair One present, Ember has been unwilling to test it to destruction.*

Under her questions, he laid out the details of the retrovirus and the projects, Ember's and Lantean, that had led this far. When he was finished, Light Breaking nodded, but Salt shook his head.

You still haven't said what it is you don't trust.

Perhaps that's because I can't put a name to it, Forge said.

Answer him, Light Breaking said, and Forge sighed.

If I can. He paused, trying to order his thoughts. *It is a clever plan,* he said at last. *A terribly clever plan, as terrible as it is clever. It could indeed solve all our problems — there are too many Wraith alive and awake, and too few humans, and by the time we can agree on who will hibernate, it will be too late. If we do this, we won't need to fight each other for the best feeding grounds — we can build on this bizarre agreement Alabaster has made with the Lanteans.*

I see Guide's hand in that, Light Breaking murmured. *But 'terrible'? Go on.*

It will change us, Forge said. *We will become — I don't know what. We will be... something different, Wraith in name and nature, but — not hunters. We will not be what we are now.*

There was a stillness between them, Light Breaking's golden eyes narrowing, and then she smiled, the rare, open smile that she shared only with the lords of her zenana. *And that is why I named you pallax, and welcomed you to my zenana. Cleverest of clevermen!*

Forge bowed deeply, knowing she could feel the pride and pleasure that swept over him.

Take the tissue samples they've shared, she went on, *and see if you can answer some of these questions that Alabaster's man is too delicate to pursue. There's enough to gain that we should go at least a little further down this road.*

As my Queen commands, Forge said, and hesitated. *Unless — will Everlasting require my assistance?*

I can't think why. My sister's folly should not be your concern. Light Breaking waved her hand in dismissal. *Find me those answers, Forge — but feed first. And rest.*

Thank you, my Queen. Forge bowed himself out of the zenana, and only when the door slid shut behind him did he realize he was not alone in the antechamber. Salt had drifted out with him, as indeterminate as the ghosts that populated his tales. Forge glanced at him, and said, emboldened by his hunger, *Is she truly so unconcerned about Moonwhite?*

Salt gave him a pained look. *Let us talk when you have fed.*

Forge started to protest, and Salt took him by the

sleeve, a terrible liberty from anyone but a storymaker.

Or at least not here.

There were drones outside the main door, easily in earshot, and the Queens of Night's lineage could control what little mind they had to share what they perceived. Forge nodded again, and they passed in silence from the Queen's chambers. Out of earshot of the watching drones, Salt paused.

You should feed, he said again.

I'm well enough for now, Forge said, though a part of him protested that it was a lie. *I would like a word or two with you.*

If you're sure, Salt said, ambiguously, and let himself be drawn into the clevermen's quarters. Forge found an unoccupied gaming room, and palmed the door closed behind them as the room's lights bloomed. In their soft radiance, Salt looked younger, more handsome, and Forge remembered again that he had been the old queen's favorite, a fixture of Light Breaking's mother's zenana. He lounged now against one of the tables, his off-hand idly caressing a handful of dice. *You're braver than most, cleverman, if you intend to ask me if the Queen is behind her sister's disappearance.*

I'm not that foolish, Forge answered, though of course it was what he had feared and they both knew it. *I would, however, like to know if there are reasons not to be concerned.*

I think she is concerned, Salt said. *Though she doesn't like to say so.*

Did you know she was here?

Salt dipped his head. *I did. Though before you ask,

I don't know why she came, and I don't know what
she wanted. They called me in to answer a question
about their mother and dismissed me again when I
had answered.*

What sort of question?

That, Salt said, with a wry grimace, *I may not tell
you.*

Forge hadn't really expected an answer. He said, *It
is unusual for any queen to have two daughters so close
in age.*

That is so. Salt's tone was cautious.

How did it happen? I have never heard the tale.

Salt hesitated but, as Forge had hoped, he seemed
unable to resist the lure of a good story. *Queen Edge
had conceived her elder daughter — she who became
Light Breaking — just as war broke out between our
hive and the hive of a Queen of Osprey called Deep
Water. We were forced to stand and fight, and to protect her daughter, Edge placed the embryo into stasis
at the heart of the hive. After the battle, she wasn't
sure if the hive had protected the embryo — we had
taken considerable damage — and so she conceived
a second daughter, she who become Moonwhite, but
couldn't bear to destroy the first. In the end, she
brought both to term, and so had two healthy daughters all but identical in age.*

And they did not quarrel, Forge said, surprised.

Salt smiled. *You sound like Edge. When the two
of them were young, they clung together, and their
mother was afraid they might not be fierce enough

to be proper queens. But as soon as they were walking, it was clear that they banded together against all others, and no one dared fight them more than once. It is not usual, I grant you, but the First Mothers did not quarrel, for all that they were nine together in the beginning.*

And yet our Queen and Moonwhite have argued for a year about this Lantean venture, Forge said. *And come no closer to an agreement.*

That is so.

Forge hesitated, not wanting to put his fears into words. It had been a brutal argument, neither queen willing to concede anything; he had been in the zenana while the sisters fought, blades and clevermen shifting uneasily, afraid to meet each other's eye in case it provoked a physical attack. Moonwhite was determined not to cooperate with the Lanteans, or any humans; Light Breaking was as determined to meet them at least halfway. Under other circumstances, the two hives would simply have parted ways, an alliance ending, but the ties of blood and a thousand years of habit were all but impossible to break. And, too, neither hive was as strong alone as they were together. It was not impossible to imagine Light Breaking deciding to end the impasse by killing her sister.

Except that if she had done so, she would surely have proclaimed it openly. Not all of Moonwhite's hive would have followed her, but many, perhaps most, would: better to follow the familiar victor than be forced to seek a new queen. Only Moonwhite's zenana would have been lost, and maybe not even all of them.

A conundrum, he said at last, and Salt bared teeth in what might have been a smile.

So it is, cleverman. So it is.

Blaze studied his queen's most likely course projected on the cruiser's navigation screen. So far, his men had managed to scan most of the planets near that line, worlds where a damaged ship could have sought refuge, and so far all of them had come up empty. Everlasting's men were searching the worlds closer to their hive, but they, too, reported no sign of the queen's scout. He tapped his claws on the edge of the console, and stilled them as the Master of Sciences Physical gave him a look. He and Icewind were not precisely rivals — in better days, they had been friends — but with the queen missing, the lords of the zenana looked first to their own security.

And still there is nothing?

You have seen everything I have, Blaze answered. He frowned at the display again. *Though there is one point that troubles me.*

Only one?

Blaze looked up sharply, but there was only wry humor in Icewind's thoughts, and he allowed himself a brief smile in return. *One that seems most pertinent.* He touched the screen, highlighting the symbol that marked Teseirit. The world's description hovered above it, a cascade of gold, and Icewind frowned curiously.

I don't see why. It looks ordinary enough.

Blaze touched the screen again, drawing a new line to the foreground. *It's very close to our queen's most likely course. But — it's on the other side of this new border Alabaster's hive has agreed to.*

Icewind hissed, thoughtfully. *And you think — what? That the Lanteans are involved?*

Blaze considered. A part of him wished it were true, an obvious enemy to throw himself against, but he could not make it make enough sense. *I don't see why they'd bother. It would be easier to control us through Alabaster rather than attack us directly, and risk angering an ally. No, what worries me is if she had any kind of problem anywhere along this section of the course —* He traced a section of the line, leaving it glowing blue. *Then Teseirit is the only place to seek shelter. There aren't any other planets within a reasonable range on our side of the border. If the scout had been damaged, I could see that it would seem a reasonable risk.*

She does not recognize that border, Icewind said, softly, and Blaze dipped his head in acknowledgement.

That had also occurred to me.

It need not provoke trouble with the Lanteans, Icewind said, after a moment. *Planets are large, and they are few in number. They need never know she was there — if indeed she's there at all.*

There's no reason to think she is, Blaze said, *except that she isn't anywhere else. And I know that between you and Rising Tide our secondary craft are in impeccable shape.* Rising Tide was the Master of Sciences Biological, responsible for growing the hulls from seed just as Icewind shaped their engines and internal systems.

Thank you for that, Icewind said, lifting his brow ridges, and Blaze suppressed a snarl.

I am not completely a fool.

Nor did I say so. Icewind made a gesture of apology. *I complain because I fear you may be right, though I can't think what would have brought her scout down. Except an attack, of course.*

And that brought them back to the glaring problem: the only other hive in this sector was Light Breaking's, and the only person who dared attack a queen was another queen.

It could be Alabaster, of course, Icewind said, after a moment.

It could, Blaze began, but could not make himself believe it. He shook his head. *It doesn't benefit her. We're no threat, she has only to push a little harder, and we will have to agree to her bargain.* It was not something he had admitted before, and he felt the same regretful certainty in Icewind's mind.

Especially since Light Breaking favors it so far.

Blaze looked back at the screen, calculating travel times and the number of Darts their smallest cruiser could carry. *We have to search,* he said.

Discreetly!

Just so. But we must be sure the scout isn't there.

If she had to set down, she would have signaled us, Icewind began, then shook his head. *Or perhaps not, knowing where she was and not wanting to draw the Lanteans' attention. You're right, we must send a cruiser.*

I'm going myself, Blaze said. It was not, strictly speaking, wise to leave the hive without queen and consort, but the Hivemaster and Icewind were more than competent. *I will take *Far-faring*, and a hand of Darts. We can scan from orbit if the Lanteans aren't there.*

And if they are? Icewind cocked his head to one side in question.

Blaze sighed. *Then, as you say, we must be exceedingly discreet.*

Far-faring was the smallest of Moonwhite's cruisers, and the youngest, grown by the Hivemaster and Rising Tide with stealth in mind. Compared to its elder sibling, it was quietly skittish, and Blaze was glad to leave flying it to the blade Whisper, who had been its pilot since its birth. That left him free to monitor the sensors as well as the ship's progress, and as they came out of hyperspace, he focused all his attention on the monitors.

Whisper brought the ship out of hyperspace into the shadow of Teseirit's larger moon and powered down immediately, hanging silent and near-invisible while the sensors probed the area around them. Blaze allowed himself a sigh of relief as one by one the probes showed nothing but empty space.

Bring us in closer. Take up station where we can monitor the Stargate.

Very well, Commander. Whisper eased *Far-faring* into motion, still under minimal power, outer lights switched off to leave the hull a rough shadow against the stars. Blaze studied the screens, searching for some sign of the scout, some signal from his queen. There was nothing, though, only the nearly endless forest that ran like a belt around the planet's equator, a thousand lakes sparkling in the light of the distant sun. There was life, the sensors could detect that much at a distance, but they were intended to identify worlds ripe for culling, not find one Wraith among a thousand humans. They would need to move closer, Blaze thought, and send out Darts as well, let them circumnavigate the planet a few times. That should be enough to pick up any traces of the queen's scout.

He started to turn away from the console, but lights flared, a warning rippling down the screen: something was rising from the planet's surface. Blaze snarled, and a second, brighter warning flared, identifying the signal as a Lantean puddle-jumper heading for orbit.

Cease all scanning! Reduce all emissions. Blaze hissed softly, watching the Lantean ship rise. If Moonwhite were here, that would certainly have brought the Lanteans to deal with a trespasser, even an unintentional one. And yet… He watched as the puddle-jumper settled into an orbit that held it stationary above the Stargate. There were a number of settlements nearby, several of them large enough to contain more than a thousand humans each. It looked almost as though the Lanteans were try- ing to provide cover, or perhaps were scanning them- selves, though if so their probe was directed at the plan- et's surface. And certainly *Far-faring* was not in orbit, nor were there any traces of debris.

Do we attack? Whisper asked, his tone doubtful. *There is only the one of them.*

The puddle-jumpers were more formidable than they looked, and besides, to attack them unprovoked would not only risk restarting hostilities with the Lanteans, but would bring Alabaster and her allies down on them as well. Blaze shook his head, still watching the screen. If Moonwhite was there, he thought hopefully, perhaps it had not been a crash. Surely the scout's sensors would have picked up the taste of debris.

I could take a single Dart. That was Red Moon, the senior Dart pilot aboard. *We are out of visual range. If I drift without power, let gravity pull me toward the surface —*

They will see you. Blaze shook his head. *We have no choice. Withdraw — keep the moon between us, and jump to hyperspace as soon as you can. We will have to find another way to search here.*

The two Consorts met on a planet its humans called Aurelis, though their scouts landed in the southern grasslands far from both the planet's Stargate and from any human settlements. They landed in twilight and met as the twin moons rose slowly in the eastern distance, one pale pink, the other gold, bright enough to cast shadows, but not so strong as to be painful to the eye. By prior agreement, Everlasting had brought only a handful of blades, plus a quartet of drones. Blaze had brought no more, and as the younger blades lobbed what passed for barbed wit at each other and their seniors began a not entirely casual game of hive-and-star, the two Consorts drew slowly apart, until they were far enough away from the ships and men that the others could not easily follow their conversation.

You found nothing either? Blaze asked. Like most of Cloud's descendants, he had wide-set eyes and broad cheekbones, his silver hair pulled up and back into an intricate double fall. As elegant as ever, Everlasting thought. They had been good friends once, before Moonwhite had seen Blaze among her sister's blades and lured him to her side. Blaze had saved his life once, when a Culling had gone wrong and Everlasting had been trapped among the human kine, and Everlasting was conscious of the debt as yet unpaid. Surely, he thought, we can remain friends still.

We did not. He shook his head for emphasis, the skirts of his coat rustling against the long grass. *Is it possible she took another course?*

Anything is possible, Blaze said, with a grim smile, *but it seems unlikely. She was determined to make this a quick visit.*

The implicit accusation hovered between them, a breath away from being uttered outright. By the scouts, a blade laughed, sharp and unamused; there was a clatter of wood on stone as another blade made a play in the game. Blaze shook his head sharply, hair whispering against the leather of his coat. It was finely worked, an embossed pattern of stars and moons above a bed of flames that flaunted his status.

I do not believe that your lady is involved in this, he said. *To speak plainly, if she intended to rid herself of her sister, I believe she would have done so openly, and come directly to the hive with an offer: join her or die.*

Everlasting hesitated for an instant, hovering on the edge of outrage, but Blaze's assessment was so close to his own that he had to nod. *That is so.*

Then who could have moved against her? Blaze took a few steps away in frustration, then turned back. *The only other queen in this sector is Alabaster. It has occurred to me that she might not be aware that —

should anything happen to our queen — we would follow Light Breaking before any other. And Moonwhite has refused to discuss this retrovirus.*

Our Master of Sciences Biological was with Alabaster's hive when Moonwhite went missing, Everlasting said. *Nothing he has said would suggest that Alabaster was involved. Though I grant you Guide is tricky.*

Even he would not go against his queen's orders, Blaze said. *I don't see what it would gain him anyway.* He paused. *You consider him trustworthy still, in spite of everything?*

I do. Everlasting didn't have to think about that question: Guide might wish to see his daughter's hive the dominant force in the galaxy, but that was honest enough. He had proved long ago that he would always keep the letter of his word, and often its spirit, even with his enemies, and that was rare in any commander, never mind one who was also Consort. *More to the point, my queen believes it, too.*

There is one final possibility that we have not been able to eliminate, Blaze said. *Teseirit lies close to my queen's most likely course, but on the Lantean side of the border Steelflower and Alabaster drew. It was in my mind that we should ask the Lanteans if we might search there.*

Everlasting cocked his head. *You haven't already done so?*

Blaze hesitated, then gave a rueful smile. *We attempted to scan from orbit, but the Lanteans were there before us. Which makes me wonder what brought them there. But before you ask, no, we didn't manage to find any answers. We withdrew as soon as we saw the Lantean ship.*

What sort of ship? Everlasting felt a chill travel down the ridge of his spine, in spite of the warm night air. If the Lanteans were coming to the borders in force...

A puddle-jumper, Blaze answered, and Everlasting hissed in relief. That could mean almost anything, from pure exploration to trade or some mission of mercy.

You're sure they didn't see you?

We took every precaution, Blaze said. *I have no desire — my queen has no desire — to provoke trouble with the Lanteans unless it is absolutely necessary.*

Everlasting considered the problem. Blaze was right, if they had searched all the other possibilities, they need to eliminate Teseirit. Moonwhite still considered it part of their shared feeding grounds, and in an emergency she wouldn't hesitate to land there. *You should ask Guide.*

What?

We should ask Guide to ask the Lanteans to let us search, Everlasting elaborated. *They're such good friends, let him do the work. And he'll do it; he wants your queen to agree to join this trial. There's a better chance they'll listen to him anyway.*

True enough. Blaze's tone was suddenly bleak with worry. *Just — hurry.*

If it were my queen, Everlasting thought, and shuddered at the idea. He touched Blaze's shoulder cautiously, as he had done when they were friends and blades together, and the other consort did not move away. *We will find her*, Everlasting thought, but they both knew it was an empty promise. *I will,* he said instead, and they turned back together toward the ships.

Light Breaking received the idea with an approving nod, and she made the connection to Alabaster herself. The other queen listened in turn, and promised to speak to the Lanteans for them, and to return their answer as soon as possible.

Which, Light Breaking added, after the connection was broken, *may mean tomorrow or next week or never. But we have done what we can.*

We should do more, Everlasting thought, but was careful not to let those words rise to the surface of his mind. He bowed instead, and backed from the zenana.

To his surprise, however, Guide himself signaled them only thirty hours later. Light Breaking received the call in the zenana, her lords about her, and Everlasting was unsurprised to see annoyance flicker across Guide's face. Guide bowed his head politely enough, however, and Light Breaking lifted her hand in a graceful welcome.

"I am glad to see you returned so soon, Guide."

"It was made clear to me that the matter was urgent," Guide answered. "And, as it happens, to more than just your hives. When we spoke to the Lanteans, they said they had found traces of Wraith activity in the system. If that is the queen Moonwhite, trespassing by accident or by pure necessity, that is one thing."

Everlasting held himself perfectly still, though he wanted to show teeth at the veiled insult. The Hivemaster hissed very softly, and Forge tilted his head to one side as though he didn't understand. Light Breaking said, "Which of course is why we wish permission to search for my sister."

"And they are willing to grant it," Guide said. "But on terms."

"I had expected no less," Light Breaking said. "Name them."

"Your party is to number no more than four," Guide said, "and it is to arrive on Teseirit by Stargate. There are to be no Wraith ships in orbit while you are on the planet. The Lanteans will meet you at the Stargate, and they will go with you as you search. And will, of course, aid you in their search."

"You can't have thought that would be acceptable," the Hivemaster said, as though the words had been startled out of him.

Light Breaking lifted her hand, though Everlasting didn't think she was actually displeased. "We must have a ship in orbit, or on the planet. How else can we search?"

"As I have said, the Lanteans have offered to put their systems at your disposal," Guide said.

"We thank them for that generous offer," Light Breaking said, "but we must be certain. And of course my sister will have every reason to conceal herself from the Lanteans, and their scanners. I am, of course, willing to send a small party."

Guide dipped his head again, and Everlasting thought he was hiding a smile. "The Lanteans were very definite —"

"So am I." Light Breaking smiled, showing teeth.

"I will carry that message back to them," Guide said, "and see if we come to some arrangement."

"I appreciate your efforts," Light Breaking said, and nodded for the Hivemaster to cut the transmission.

Distant Thunder, the Master of Sciences Physical, snarled openly as soon as the screen went blank. *He overreaches.*

Light Breaking turned to fix him with a stare, but the cleverman held his ground.

It is not his place, Lady, even if he was Consort once and is now the Queen's acknowledged sire. He has no right to dictate terms.

I would rather deal with him than Alabaster, Light Breaking said. *There's a bit more room to maneuver. Everlasting. If they agree, who should we send?*

Blaze must go, Everlasting answered. It was his right as Consort to the missing queen, and it had been his idea in the first place. *And I would want to join him. With your permission, Lady.*

I will consider it, Light Breaking answered. *In the meantime, who else?*

Surely Blaze will want to choose men of his own, the Hivemaster said.

Indeed he may, but I will claim at least one more place, Light Breaking answered.

Forge, Distant Thunder said. *Blaze cannot think him involved, he was on Alabaster's hive. And his skills may be useful.*

Well, cleverman? Light Breaking looked at the Master of Sciences Biological, who bowed deeply.

If my Lady wishes it, of course I will go. He straightened. *And will we provide the ship to take us to the nearest Stargate? I can't think Guide will like it if we each send one.*

That, Light Breaking said, *is something Blaze and

I will need to discuss.* She waved a hand in dismissal. *But first the Lanteans must agree to our request. Go now, my lords, but be ready.*

The lords of the zenana filed out obediently. Everlasting hung toward the rear, hoping that the queen would signal him to stay, but she made no move, and at last he bowed himself out with the rest. He found himself at Forge's side, and the cleverman slid an arm through his before he could move away.

I would like a moment.

Everlasting let himself be drawn aside into one of the chambers grown for the clevermen. It was pleasant enough, softly lit, mist coiling up from the corners, and in spite of himself he felt some of the tension leave his shoulders. Forge dropped onto one of the several couches, graceful without deliberate airs, and said, *I don't want to go.*

Everlasting had been about to seat himself, and checked abruptly. He made himself move again, settling himself comfortably against the long shaped cushions, and said, *Why not?*

Forge raised his brow ridges at that. *I am a cleverman, not a blade. And this is not a matter that will be settled by science.*

It might yet be, Everlasting answered. *Our queen is right; Moonwhite will be hiding from the Lanteans' sensors as much as from the Lanteans themselves. And Distant Thunder is right, too. You, at least, could not be involved in any conspiracy.*

And I presume there is none? Forge tipped his head to one side.

I could take that as an insult.

None was intended, as you well know. Forge paused. *Let me speak openly.*

Everlasting nodded.

If Moonwhite is dead, the most likely hand behind it is our queen's. We all know this — you would not otherwise even think of sending me. Can you tell me that you know nothing of this?

I know nothing more than you, Everlasting said. *I give you my word on that.*

For a long moment, Forge didn't move, but then his lips curved into a wry smile. *I believe you. And I think that worries me even more.*

Blaze stood in his queen's empty zenana, the throne gleaming white at its center. If Moonwhite were truly lost… It was a thought that made him shudder, and he was glad there was no one else there to see. But it had to be faced, the worst possibility of all. If she were lost by accident, some terrible mischance, Light Breaking would take her sister's people into her hive. She might eventually breed them a queen of their own again, as it would be a shame to waste a hiveship on a queenless crew. She might even welcome him, who had once been of her faction, potential pallax and lord of her zenana, and he did not know what to think of that. In time, the grief would wear away, and he might welcome that favor, but now the possibility grated, irked him like sand on raw flesh. But if Light Breaking were behind the attack, he could not join her hive — he couldn't stand against her either, not when most of the hive would rather serve

Moonwhite's sister than a stranger. Sorocide was the rule among Wraith, and the sisters' friendship the exception, but he would not serve her. Though surely if the sisters had fallen out over policy, Light Breaking would have proclaimed the deed, and demanded the hive's allegiance. That thought was perversely reassuring, and he took a steadying breath. And if Alabaster were behind this… That was the real unknown factor, the blank face on the die, the counter that shifted from ten to none depending on its place on the board. Even together, the two hives could not stand against her, not with Guide standing in for the consort and the Lantean alliance in place. And yet — if she wanted their hunting grounds, she didn't need to risk even the sort of attack they could make. Neither Moonwhite nor Light Breaking would have fought, not if Alabaster had pressed her demands. And that brought him back to the possibility of accident, of catastrophic drive failures and breached hulls, all the one-in-a-million chance that went with space travel. It was possible for a ship to vanish, and have no one ever learn its fate.

But he was not there yet, and with a bit of luck, might never be. A chime sounded, drawing his eyes to the unlit screen set into the rear wall, and a voice spoke over the ship's intercom. "Commander. The queen's sister wishes to speak with you."

"Put her through." Blaze straightened his spine and turned to face the screen as it came to life, displaying Light Breaking's well-remembered face. "Lady."

"Guide has spoken with the Lanteans," she said, "and they have made us an offer."

"Will they let us search?"

"On terms."

Blaze hissed softly. That was better than he had hoped, and the relief was almost painful. "What terms?"

"Only four Wraith may land on the planet, and they must be escorted by the Lanteans. We have persuaded them to let us put a small cruiser in orbit so that we may search more efficiently, but they are adamant about the rest."

Blaze nodded. "We should send *Far-faring* — it's the smallest of all our cruisers, but still carries a full complement of Darts."

"And is yours," Light Breaking said, but the words held no heat. "But, yes, it is the smallest, and I agree it should be the one we send. But I also want to name men to the party."

"I intend to go myself, of course," Blaze said. "And I would not object to bringing one of your people with me."

"Everlasting," Light Breaking said, "and also Forge." She lifted a hand before he could protest. "Forge cannot have been involved in any plot, and he is my Master of Sciences Biological as well as pallax. He is my pledge to you that I have nothing to do with this."

Blaze bowed deeply. "Thank you, Lady. I will be glad of his company." He didn't have to pretend sincerity: he had known Forge before the two hives split, and knew his temperament; besides, if the queen's scout was badly damaged, his skills would come in useful.

"And your second?"

Blaze hesitated. There were a dozen blades he could choose, any one of whom would leap at the chance to serve their queen. But he and Everlasting were both just as competent, and if he could only bring one more, it should be someone whose skills were unique. "Salt."

Light Breaking tilted her head as though he had surprised her. "The storymaker?"

"My queen knows and trusts him," Blaze answered, "and he has never declared himself for either of you above the other. That is my pledge of trust."

She nodded slowly. "That is — wise, I think. Very well, if he will go, I will name him to the Lanteans."

"He'll go," Blaze said. The storymaker wouldn't refuse to help either daughter of the queen he had served.

"I expect he will," Light Breaking answered, and broke the connection.

Salt had no true home on either hive, though a portion of the guest quarters was permanently at his disposal on both ships. For an instant, waking in the quiet dark, he could not remember which ship he inhabited at the moment, which queen he presently sought to entertain, but then the memory came rushing back. He snarled and waved for the lights to brighten. He could see no good ending at the moment, and that fear wakened the grief of his old loss, Edge raven-haired as her daughters, and twice as daring. That daring had been her death, as he had always known it would be. That it had taken their son — his impossible, unlikely son; storymakers might share a queen's bed, but did not provide her children — as well was an added sorrow.

He put those thoughts away, and uncurled from his nest, then reached for the clothes that had been left for him. Edge's daughters had extended him many of the privileges of a Queen-father, since Edge had never formally chosen a Consort, and the blades of her zenana had been an ever-changing group. In truth, she had preferred clevermen, being herself too like a blade in temperament; her Masters of Sciences had been her most constant companions, though they had not fathered daughters. Salt had outlived them both, Dustwind lost with Edge, and Jewelbright killed shepherding the daughters' long retreat, as he had outlived most of his generation: he was willing to accept those courtesies that eased his way. In truth, it was probably time he went looking for an apprentice — the habit of mind that made a storymaker was uncommon, a happy accident rather than a talent planned and bred for. Certainly both Light Breaking and Moonwhite were too young to expend fertility on such indulgence. They needed more blades and clevermen, and daughters to continue their lines, far more than they needed odder talents. No, he thought, fastening the line of tiny clasps that closed his second-best coat, he would need to look to one of the larger hives, with a well-established queen and the time and leisure to breed more than the most necessary children. After Death's attempt to bring all Wraith under her rule, those were few and far between, and he allowed himself a sigh of regret. When he was young, the Ancients had been gone for a thousand years, and the galaxy had been filled with queens worthy of service…

And if he was succumbing to nostalgia in his old age, it was long past time to find an apprentice, and then he could retire to the core of the hive and grow old and toothless in its embrace. He snarled at his own fancies,

and glanced at his image in the mirror the hive shaped
for him. The Wraith who looked back at him was tall
and lean, well past maturity but still handsome according to the canon of Osprey, light-boned and strong. He
had given up the most elaborate hairstyles with Edge's
death — there had seemed to be no reason to bother, in
those bleak days — and now he tidied the long fall into
a single silver braid. He flexed his fingers thoughtfully,
and the door slid back to reveal one of the young to-be-
blades who served as messengers.

*Your pardon, but the queen would like to speak with
you.*

That was not surprising, given the negotiations. *I am
at her disposal,* Salt said, conventionally, and followed
the boy through the maze of corridors to the zenana.

Light Breaking was there alone, and that was surprising enough that Salt found himself looking from side to
side as though Everlasting might suddenly appear from
the shadows. Light Breaking bared teeth at him.

I wished to speak to you, not to my consort.

Salt bowed, spreading his hands. *And here I am,
Lady.*

She stared at him for a long moment, not entirely
mollified, and then with an effort relaxed against her
throne. *We have come to terms with the Lanteans. We
will be sending a cruiser to Teseirit — well, Blaze will,
his *Far-faring* is better suited to the business than either
of mine — and four men will be allowed to accompany
the Lanteans on the planet. I am sending Everlasting and
Forge, and Blaze has requested that you be his second.*

Salt lifted his head, startled. *Why?* He could think

of a dozen more likely men, blades and clevermen both.

He says it is a token of his good intentions, Light Breaking said, with a thin smile. *You were my mother's man — you are still hers, in many ways, which does not trouble me. You have never favored me over my sister or her over me, and I believe you will not do it now.*

I am a storymaker, Lady. What can I do that a blade cannot do better?

Light Breaking paused, her thoughts momentarily shuttered. *My sister loves you,* she said at last, *as I love you. If someone has persuaded her that I mean her harm —*

Salt looked up sharply. *So that is what you fear.*

Among other things. Can you tell me I am unreasonable?

Salt shook his head. He had seen that sort of manipulation in other hives, and to a lesser degree among the blades vying for Edge's favor. *Lady, I cannot.*

Light Breaking sighed. *She will trust you. And I trust you. Bring my sister back.*

If I can, Salt answered, and they both knew it for a vow.

CHAPTER TWO

GUIDE had promised to perform the introductions himself, and so his scout emerged from hyperspace over Teseirit only a heartbeat after *Far-faring*. Everlasting suppressed a snarl — having to depend on the wily old commander set his nerves on edge even before they had to deal with the Lanteans — but Blaze merely nodded as the comm screen lit to reveal Guide's face. He looked like a mere blade, his hair loose and disheveled, the star tattooed around one eye very dark against his pale skin, but no one, Everlasting thought, was deceived.

"If you are ready, you may come aboard."

Everlasting did snarl this time, and Forge cocked his head to one side as though he were curious. Salt smiled in what looked like genuine amusement. Blaze ignored them all, and said, "We will."

"The Lanteans are waiting."

"Then we will not delay," Blaze said, patiently enough, but even so it was a good hour before the heavily-laden scout descended to the makeshift landing site, the passenger compartment crowded with their party and Guide's men. They were at one end of the long clearing that held the Stargate, at the opposite end from the gate platform itself, and the ground between was covered with knee-high grass and starred with flowers. The sun was past the zenith, but its light was bright enough to make Everlasting wince and narrow his eyes, and he felt Forge flinch. Guide lifted a brow ridge at them.

Surely a little sunlight doesn't hurt.

Forge controlled his thoughts with an effort, but Salt laughed aloud. *Of course it hurts, Commander, and you'll suffer with us. Still, lead on.*

Guide stiffened, though he had more self-control than to show even a hint of teeth, but then he released breath in a sound that was not quite a hiss. *Salt. And why would your queen send a jester, I wonder?*

I've known Moonwhite since she was a child just walking, Salt answered, as though it were a real question. *And Light Breaking, too. And of course, I can bear witness.*

And that was the sting in the tail. No one could have said more plainly or more unobjectionably that Guide was hardly impartial in the matter. Everlasting curbed his own delight, and said, *The Lanteans are waiting, Commander.*

After you, Guide answered, and they made their way down the ramp and out into the grasses.

The sun was hot, dazzling even after his pupils had contracted to hairline slits, and he saw the distant movement before the shapes came clear. There were four Lanteans as well, one large male, two smaller males, and a slender female walking just behind one of the smaller males. Guide lifted his hand, signaling both greeting and for his group to stop, and Everlasting lifted his head, letting the breeze carry any trace chemicals past his sensor pits. He could taste humans, certainly, and not much more — none of the fear that usually flared when humans faced Wraith, though he could also taste a cold and underlying anger, like the tang of iron and blood. Forge felt it, too, and hissed softly.

The big one is dangerous…

They are all dangerous, Guide said. *And you would do well to remember it.* He stepped forward as the Lanteans came within earshot. "Sheppard! We are here as agreed."

The male in the lead nodded in answer, though he did not take his hands from the ugly Lantean weapon slung across his chest. Everlasting eyed it uneasily. He had never faced those weapons, though like all Wraith he had heard about them: a gunpowder weapon, but only vaguely like the ones used on Sateda and Hoff and among the Genii, one that spat bullets fast enough to overwhelm even a fully-fed Wraith's ability to heal. All four of them carried those weapons, and for the first time Everlasting felt a thread of fear worm its way down his spine. The Lanteans might be even more deadly than people had claimed.

"Guide. So these are the guys who lost their queen?"

Blaze bared teeth at that, and even Salt looked shocked. Everlasting wondered if the insult had been deliberate.

"They are." Guide extended his off hand, naming them one by one. "This is Blaze, Consort to Moonwhite who is missing. Everlasting, Consort of Light Breaking. Forge, Master of Sciences Biological to Light Breaking. And Salt — storymaker."

The one called Sheppard fixed Blaze with a hard stare. He was a tall man, with dark hair showing the first signs of gray at the temples: a senior blade, then. "Guide says you think your queen might be here."

Blaze said carefully, "As I am sure Guide has told you,

our queen disappeared while traveling between our hive and her sister's, and we believe it is possible that she may have crash landed here. That is why we have asked permission to search."

"You sure you didn't take a quick look first?" That was the big man. He was darker than the others, and his hair hung in the same kind of heavy cords that were popular with the Wraith of Night's lineage. That similarity was vaguely disturbing, and Everlasting looked away.

"We are aware of the borders set out in the agreement," Blaze said, still speaking with great care. "And, though my queen has not formally assented to this treaty, it was still her wish that we honor it while we considered."

"Like that's believable," the big man said, not quite softly enough to ignore.

"Ronon." That was the female, stepping forward to take her place beside Sheppard. She was small and dark and sharp of feature, and Forge drew breath sharply.

That is the Young Queen. And the Consort. Which Guide did not see fit to mention.

It is they indeed, Guide answered, *and surely it's better to deal with them than with some underling.*

I would have liked to know that we had drawn their notice, Blaze said.

The Young Queen went on as though they had not spoken — though of course, Everlasting thought, she could not hear their normal mode of communication. "Though he has a point. Our allies here have said they saw Wraith ships in the night sky."

"Which might be a sign that my queen did come here," Blaze said, "and may be stranded anywhere on the planet."

"I'm willing to bet your cruiser already scanned for her," Sheppard said.

This time Blaze did show teeth. "Of course."

"And?"

"We have no conclusive readings," Blaze answered.

"Oh, come on!" That was the third male, the one who had not yet spoken. "We know there have been Wraith here —"

"Rodney," the Young Queen said, and in almost the same moment, Sheppard said, "McKay…"

"Well, we do." The one called McKay glared at both of them.

"This is news to me," Guide said.

"We hadn't locked down all the details," Sheppard answered. "But, yeah, you might say we have proof that you people have been here."

The Young Queen took another step forward. "There has been an outbreak of blood fever in one of the perimeter villages. So far, it has spread to four more. We have sent medical aid, of course, but there have already been deaths, and are likely to be more."

"And we all know," Ronon said, "that the Wraith spread the blood fever."

In spite of himself, Everlasting took a half step backwards. Blood fever was one of the few diseases that had adapted to prey on the Wraith, and, while it was not invariably fatal, it was dangerous enough — and contagious enough — that most hives went out of their way to avoid it, even to the extent of abandoning an infected hunting ground for a generation or two.

"We are also vulnerable to it," Forge said. "And if you have come from an infected area, you endanger us all."

Even Guide looked concerned at that, and Ronon smiled. "That's got you worried –"

"Only a fool would not be," Forge snapped.

"Ronon," the Young Queen said again. She fixed Forge with a hard stare. "We have taken all precautions. You are safe — unlike the people of the surrounding villages who have already been exposed, and who do not have easy access to our medicines."

"And there's one more thing that doesn't make us very happy," Sheppard said. "We've got our doctors working on treatment, and they think this is an engineered disease."

But that's nonsense, Forge protested. He shook his head, and spoke aloud. "That is — I grant you, it's not impossible, but it is highly unlikely. It is too dangerous to our own hives. No cleverman with half a brain would create a strain of that bacterium."

"Beckett thinks maybe you were trying to make it work just on humans," McKay said.

"I doubt that's possible," Forge said.

"Why would we believe you?" Ronon asked, and this time, the Young Queen did not correct him.

"This is hardly relevant to our problem," Blaze said, and fixed his stare on Sheppard. "If our queen is here, she is in grave danger. Let us search for her. If she isn't here, we'll search elsewhere."

"And if she is?" Sheppard's smile had no real amusement in it.

"We will recover her and leave," Blaze answered.

"Having infected the entire planet!" McKay exclaimed.

"McKay." Sheppard shook his head. "It seems like one hell of a coincidence that Teseirit gets hit with an outbreak of blood fever when you guys are sniffing around our borders."

"We have kept our part of the treaty," Everlasting said, controlling his anger with an effort. "Even though we were not part of it, nor were we consulted by those queens who signed it, we have honored their word to our own disadvantage. We require similar good faith from you if this treaty is to continue."

He felt the heat of Guide's annoyance wash over him, feeling without words, and saw Sheppard's hands tighten on his weapon. Ronon was smiling, the look of a blade ready and eager for combat, and the Young Queen was expressionless. Sheppard said, "Before we go any further, we'd like some assurance that these hives — Blaze and Everlasting — aren't actually responsible for our problems. That's assurance from you, Guide."

Guide spread his hands, deliberately showing the hand-mouth. "And what would you consider sufficient assurances, Sheppard?"

"I want proof that this isn't a Wraith-engineered disease."

"We are here in good faith," Blaze said.

Ronon snorted. Sheppard said, stubbornly, "We want proof."

Forge looked at Guide. "How, Commander, are we

supposed to answer this? What have you brought us into?"

"An excellent question," Blaze said.

"It is indeed," Guide answered, "and one I turn back on you, Sheppard. I know nothing of this, nor — I believe — do my allies. So how are we supposed to answer?"

"Well, I'd like the truth," Sheppard answered, "but I'll settle for something a bit more… plausible than this. Get Dr. Keller to certify what we've found."

That is the Fair One? Salt asked, and Guide nodded.

"There is no time," Blaze said. "To bring her here — you put our queen's life even more at risk by the delay."

"That's not really our concern," Sheppard said.

Everlasting bared teeth at that, but Forge spoke first. "If this is in fact accurate — if someone is trying to turn the blood fever into a weapon — we also need to know as much about it as possible. And it is also possible that your scientist has — misunderstood — the evidence. Or possibly it is something left over from the fight with Queen Death. We know her people made many regrettable choices. Let me examine the evidence."

"You've got to be kidding me," McKay said.

"It is indeed possible that this is engineered by the Wraith but not by these hives," the Young Queen said, with a glance at Sheppard. "If Forge is willing to consult with Dr. Beckett, perhaps that would be the quickest solution to our problem."

"If Forge does this, will you let us search?" Blaze asked.

Everlasting held his breath. That was the key, the one thing they needed. The Young Queen and Sheppard locked eyes a moment longer, and then Sheppard nodded.

"Ok. But just him."

Are you willing? Blaze looked over his shoulder, his own eagerness palpable.

I will go, Forge answered, and one corner of his mouth curled up in a wry smile. *And trust you to come for me if there is treachery.*

I will promise that, Everlasting said, his tone grim, and Forge dipped his head.

"I will go with you," he said aloud, and Sheppard nodded.

"Then let's get on with it."

The Lanteans had set up their field lab in the village nearest the Stargate. It was a long walk, particularly in the sun and painful light, and the skin of Forge's back tingled each time Ronon dropped behind him. He stiffened his spine and pretended he felt nothing, but he didn't think any of the Lanteans were deceived. They had taken over one of the few stone buildings, a small outbuilding belonging to the central hall, and there was a generator outside to provide lights and power as well as hastily-applied plastic sheeting over the windows. Sheppard paused by the door and looked at the Young Queen.

"You introduce him to Beckett. McKay and I need a word with the mayor."

Forge blinked at the direct order, but the Young Queen merely nodded. Perhaps they had misunderstood which Queen Sheppard served?

"I'll go with you," Ronon said, with another of his blade's smiles.

"As you wish," the Young Queen answered. "But remember that Forge has work to do."

"And I'll make sure that's all he does," Ronon answered.

The Young Queen gestured toward the door. "This way, please."

Forge hesitated, every nerve screaming that this was a trap, that he would push open that door to feel a hail of bullets that would overwhelm his ability to heal — or, worse, merely incapacitate him long enough for the Lanteans to imprison him securely. To be trapped, examined and starved until one thing or the other killed him... His hands knotted, claws flexing, and it took all his willpower to relax and step forward. The Lanteans would gain nothing by such a betrayal; they were canny folk, but neither stupid nor willfully cruel. He was safe enough for now.

Inside the little building, it was cooler and less bright, and the Lanteans had filled the space with their machines. A dark-haired male looked up from one of the computers, his eyebrows drawing together in an unhappy frown, and a thin female rose to her feet, looking worried. They were both unarmed, but there were a pair of the Lantean soldiers on watch, both carrying the ugly gunpowder weapons.

"This is Forge," the Young Queen said, in a voice that was at once serene and still brooked no disagreement. "We have agreed that he should look at your research, Dr. Beckett."

"Oh, aye?" The man's frown deepened. "And why?"

"Their queen is missing," the Young Queen said.

"Not my queen," Forge said, in spite of himself. The

Lanteans all looked at him in confusion. "She who is missing is the sister of my queen —" There was no sign of comprehension in the humans' expressions. "I have been told that you believe this blood fever to be an artificial outbreak."

The man called Beckett nodded. "Aye, and a Wraith creation at that."

"I would like to see your evidence."

"And I repeat, why?"

Forge swallowed an angry response that he knew was born of fear, the Lantean weapons that could kill him outright without effort and Ronon's looming presence at his back. "Because I cannot imagine that any of us would be so foolish as to attack any human colony with a weapon that could so easily turn against us. We are also vulnerable to the blood fever."

Beckett eyed him for a moment longer. "All right, come and take a look — that's what you wanted, Teyla?"

The Young Queen nodded again. "It is."

"Right," Beckett said. "Here's what we have so far."

Forge started toward the computer, and heard Ronon move behind him. He swung around, teeth not quite bared, to see the big man's blaster trained on him.

"I won't kill him," Ronon said, to the Young Queen, who gave a thin smile.

"Very well."

A stunner was better than the Lantean weapons, Forge told himself, and turned his attention to Beckett, though his skin crawled with fear. "Show me."

Beckett typed something into his computer, and the screen filled with Lantean symbols and small schematic drawings. Forge shook his head. "I can't read your writing. Have you no direct images?"

Beckett touched keys again, and the first drawing expanded until it filled the screen. "This is what we've worked out."

Forge considered the image, picking out the shape of the molecules and the projected bonds between them. He could see why Beckett thought this strain had been manipulated, could almost believe that certain changes were hooks deliberately set — to make the fever more virulent? To make it more aggressive toward humans? Both were possible, but the structure did not quite fit. "May I see your original sample? How have you cultured it?"

"We haven't," Beckett said shortly. "It's too risky to keep live samples here."

Forge lifted his brow ridges in surprise — he had not expected that precaution, though he supposed it wasn't unreasonable, given the primitive nature of the building — and then focused his attention on the new images that swam into focus in the screen. This was more like it, the actual virus displayed in its natural shapes, some stained by Lantean preparations to highlight internal structure, some left untouched as a control. Here it was easy to see where the mutation had been encouraged, shaped the way a Hivemaster pruned flesh and bone to speed the growth of a useful ship, and his lips pulled back from his teeth. "Yes," he said aloud, "I see what you have seen. This is not my work, nor, I am certain, the work of my counterpart in Moonwhite's hive — I would know his hand if I saw it."

"But would you say so?" Beckett asked.

"As you please, of course," Forge answered, and looked at the Young Queen. "But I will remind you that we are here in search of our queen's sister, and have done so abiding by an agreement to which we were not even party."

The Young Queen dipped her head at that. Beckett said, "If you didn't do it, then, who did, and why?"

"Who I cannot guess," Forge answered, and bent close to the screen again. Beckett worked a control, expanding the image, and Forge nodded his thanks. "I do not recognize the hand, not that I would expect to unless it were a lab-mate of mine. Why, though…" He considered the pattern of mutation, the tiny clues embedded in the magnified cells. "I do not think this was an attempt to make the blood fever deadly to humans only. First, if that were so, I would have expected this unknown cleverman to have begun here —" He touched the screen, indicating the protein spikes that jutted from the icosahedral center. "That is the point of infection for both Wraith and human, and there are sufficient differences in our genetics that it should be possible to find a protein that accesses a receptor we do not share. Instead, the changes are to the nucleic acid. I think any difference in the infection rate between species was an unintended byproduct."

"Then what was the intention?" Beckett asked.

"I would need to run tests," Forge answered, "but to my eyes, it seems as though this is intended to be a more deadly strain. And that — it makes no sense."

"It kills humans," Ronon said.

Forge looked deliberately at the bared skin at the base

of the big man's neck. "We do not want you dead. Not until we have drunk our fill."

"Actually, that does make a kind of sense," Beckett said hastily, and Forge turned back to him.

"Thank you for saying so."

"The question then is why anyone would create a disease that was not only deadly to their own species, but destroyed their food supply," the Young Queen said. "And I think we all have an answer to that."

Beckett gave a grim nod, and Forge said, "The queen who called herself Death. She was determined to force all hives into a dependence on her alone —" He stopped then, wondering if he had said too much, but the Young Queen nodded in agreement. And surely the Lanteans had learned that much during their alliance with Guide.

"The big question is how it got here," Ronon said.

"Through the Stargate, perhaps," Forge countered.

"Highly unlikely," Beckett said. "The first cases occurred in villages several hundred kilometers from the gate, and when we arrived with treatment, there were only a handful of cases here. This village is closest to the gate."

"I'm betting the Wraith brought it," Ronon said, to the Young Queen. "If they've lost a ship — and a queen — that means they could just have been sick, they didn't even have to have brought the fever here on purpose."

It was just barely possible, Forge thought. Moonwhite had not been sick when she visited her sister, but this more virulent strain might have a shorter incubation period, and queen and crew might have been overcome on their way back to their own hive. Which could mean that his own hive was in danger — or that Light Breaking had deliberately infected her sister. He shoved that thought away. If Light Breaking were behind her sister's death, she would have claimed it openly. He had to believe that. "Perhaps. Moonwhite was well when she left our hive, but — it could be. And that is all the more reason to find her as quickly as we can. Though we are all at risk of infection."

"Dr. Beckett has developed a vaccine," the Young Queen said. "We are not at risk."

"*We* are." Forge suppressed a snarl.

"You'd — I'd be willing to let you take the injection," Beckett said, "but frankly I've no idea if it would work. Or what else it might do."

"We have no time for that," Forge said. He shook his head. "Let me take supplies for this treatment you have developed, just in case. Otherwise — we will have to take our chances."

The Lanteans returned to the field beside the Stargate a few hours later, as the sun approached the zenith. The Wraith had retreated to the shelter of the trees that edged the clearing, glad of the shade that cut the light, but when Blaze saw the figures coming across the field, he gathered the others with a glance.

They are returning.

And Forge is well, I see, Everlasting answered, with some asperity. He was fond of the cleverman, Blaze knew, as well as an ally.

Let's hope they've found something useful, Salt said, with a glance at Guide, and the group made their way out into the blinding light.

"Blaze!" Sheppard lifted a hand briefly, but returned it almost at once to the stock of his weapon. "We're willing to help you search for this missing queen."

"We are grateful," Blaze said. He glanced once at Forge, who met his eyes squarely.

They're right, the virus has been modified. I fear it is Death's work. The Lanteans have developed a treatment which they have shared with us — and they have a vaccine for themselves — but we should be cautious.

Blaze heard Everlasting hiss softly, and barely kept himself from showing teeth. *And our queen?*

No sign of her. The one called McKay has a possible search vector.

Blaze took a breath and made himself focus on Sheppard again. "We have an area we would like to investigate first."

"McKay's got some ideas, too," Sheppard said. He gave his wary smile. "I'll be interested to see how they line up."

"And I will take the opportunity to leave you at this point," Guide said.

"And here I thought you'd want to come along," Sheppard said.

Guide shook his head. "This is not my concern, though of course my queen takes some interest. I have performed the introductions. The rest is up to you."

For a moment, it looked as though Ronon was going to protest, but Sheppard said, "Suit yourself. We'll let you know what happens."

"I have no doubt that I will hear the story," Guide answered, with an oblique smile, and turned back to the scout. *We will wait in orbit until you return.*

Blaze took a deep breath, knowing better than to reveal his anger, though he suspected Guide could feel it well enough. "Let us see how our ideas compare," he said aloud, and McKay reached for a laptop.

The Lanteans had identified the same area as the most likely starting point for a search, and Blaze didn't know whether to take that as a good sign or not. Still, it was a step closer to finding his queen, and if Forge was right about the blood fever… He put that thought aside. He would find Moonwhite as quickly as possible: there was no other choice.

The Lanteans, after some brief low-voiced discussion that even Blaze's sharp ears could not follow, urged them aboard one of their small scout craft — jumpers, he remembered they were called. The four Wraith settled themselves unhappily in the rear compartment, flanked by the soldiers the Lanteans called "Marines" with gunpowder weapons trained on them, and Sheppard and McKay took their places at the pilots' stations.

"It would be best if you sat very still," the Young Queen said, from the seat directly behind Sheppard, and Blaze thought it would be wise to obey. Still, they were at least free to talk and he glanced sideways at Salt, who to his surprise was looking almost ill.

What's wrong?

I haven't seen a ship like this since I was a child, Salt said. *It brings back… memories. That's all.*

Forge, Everlasting said. *Do you know how they identified this area? Did someone see a ship go down?*

They didn't tell me, Forge answered, *but I think

they are tracking backward from the first reports of the blood fever.* He gave Blaze an apologetic look. *They believe we are responsible for the outbreak.*

That's impossible, Blaze began, and stopped. It wasn't impossible, of course, not if Light Breaking had betrayed her sister. Moonwhite had not shared her reasons for this visit, hasty and secret as it was. It was easy to imagine some thought, some question, posed to lure Moonwhite to Light Breaking's hive, where she could be exposed to the virus and sent on her way before she could endanger any of her sister's people... But, no, Light Breaking had not claimed either a death or her sister's hive, and he refused to believe that she would prolong the process.

There was no sickness on your hive, surely? Everlasing asked, tentatively.

Nothing, Blaze answered. Unless, of course, there had been an outbreak after he had left — but the fever would have shown itself before, the incubation period was known and long past. He rested his head against the padded bulkhead, unable to make sense of any of this.

There could not be, Forge said, almost in the same moment, *or we would have shown signs of illness, too. And that is proof against the Lanteans' theory: if your queen were contagious, our people would be sick as well.*

You said the virus was modified, Salt began, and Forge shook his head, drawing an abortive movement from the nearest Marine.

"It's all right, Hernandez," the Young Queen said, and the man subsided. She seemed remarkably calm, and for an instant Blaze wondered if she somehow understood their conversation. But that was impossible, and he shook himself back to the business at hand.

Yes, but not in a way that would prolong the incubation period, Forge said. *Or at least, not that I could see in the Lantean samples, as much as I was allowed to examine them. But the fact that it seems more virulent would also tend to rule out a longer incubation.*

That was certainly true, Blaze thought, and tried to convince himself it was encouraging. If Moonwhite were truly lost... He had come to her mother's hive as a young blade, knowing only that his own hive was overpopulated with ambitious blades and clevermen, and that someday the daughters would have hives of their own. He had not aspired then to any queen's favor, not until he had seen the sisters side by side in the hive's great atrium, laughing together at the words of some other blade. They were both beautiful, with jet black hair that made their skin look the paler by contrast, and the full breasts and broad hips of the daughters of Night, both beautiful and clever, skilled leaders. Light Breaking was the more outspoken of the pair, and she had been quick to catch the eye of both Forge and Everlasting, but Blaze himself had been drawn to Moonwhite's quieter certainties. She said less, and took more time to say it, but she chose more wisely than Light Breaking.

He buried that thought, not wanting to offend either Forge or Everlasting — he and Everlasting had been good friends, once, before their choices led them down different paths — but Salt slanted a glance at him anyway, and he caught a hint of the storymaker's rueful approval.

"Where are you taking us?" he asked aloud, hoping to distract the others, and Ronon turned in his seat, showing very white teeth.

"A little late to be worrying about that."

Forge dipped his head to hide a wry smile, and Everlasting said, *That one is beginning to get on my nerves.*

"We are tracking back along the vector of infection," the Young Queen began, and in the co-pilot's seat McKay sat up sharply.

"Hey. I've — yes, we've got something."

Everlasting made an abortive movement, and relaxed again as the Marines raised their weapons. Blaze repressed the desire to lean forward, to peer through the jumper's windshield, and said, carefully, "What have you found?"

"Traces of organic compounds," McKay answered, "burnt wood, turpenes —"

"A wrecked Wraith scout," Sheppard said. "And there's a village not far away."

Blaze suppressed a hiss. If Moonwhite or her blades had been injured, they would have needed to feed, and the village would be the closest food source. From the looks on the Marines' faces, they had made the same calculation, and didn't like the results.

This may be... unfortunate, Salt said.

"Are there any signs of life?" Blaze asked aloud. He would not apologize, or offer excuses, not until he knew that there was something to excuse.

"Nothing so far," McKay answered. "Well, I mean, not Wraith, and not at the wreck site, but there are people in the village —"

The jumper tilted and circled, and this time Blaze

did hiss as he saw the crumpled shape that had been the scout *Nimble*. It had come down more or less under control, he thought, but the ground here was rough, rising from foothills to impressive mountains, and the scout had burrowed its nose and one lifting surface into the broken terrain, leaving a gouged track and shreds of hide and bracing in the shattered trees. It was dead — mercifully, with that damage — and he could not spare it the regret it deserved.

I do not feel Moonwhite, Salt said, his eyes focusing on nothing.

Nor I, Blaze answered, and said aloud, "And our queen?"

"I'm not seeing any Wraith," Sheppard answered. His hands moved busily over the controls. "We're going to check out the village."

The jumper swung away, skimming the dark treetops. Blaze leaned forward just a little, heedless of the Marines, and saw a clearing ahead. At its far end, there was a cluster of woven-grass roofs: the village, then, and its fields. Sheppard circled once, and then brought the jumper down easily near the clearing's edge.

"Stay right there," the nearest Marine said, and the jumper's rear door folded neatly down. The air that swept in was cooler than in the lowlands, and smelled of crushed grass and smoke. Blaze frowned at that, and saw Forge's head lift.

What has burned —

"Ok, on your feet," Sheppard interrupted. "Walk out, and keep your hands where I can see them."

Blaze felt Everlasting's rising anger and said quickly,

"Yes. We will do so." He suited his actions to his word, rising carefully and walking down the ramp with his spine held perfectly straight, hands open and empty at his side. Forge copied him, and Everlasting followed with more reluctance, but Salt looked, if anything, faintly amused.

"So this is one of the outlier villages," he said aloud, lifting his head so that the breeze stirred the tip of his long braid. "But where are the villagers?"

It was a fair question, Blaze thought, and saw the Marines exchange nervous glances. There was, at first glance, only a handful of buildings, one larger than the rest and set toward the edge of the clearing, four other, smaller houses with conical roofs, and a fenced enclosure that ran from the smallest house almost to the woods. The air smelled even more strongly of burning, but no smoke rose from any of the buildings. The fenced enclosure was empty even of animals, and there was no sign of humans anywhere.

One of the houses has burned, Everlasting said, and tilted his head. Blaze looked more closely, and realized that what he had taken for a pile of rubbish was in fact the remains of another hut.

"Looks like there was a fire," Ronon said, in the same instant, and the young Queen lifted her head.

"There." She pointed, and the others turned to look as a thin figure rose out of the grass, waving a strip of scarlet cloth.

"Stay back!" it called. "Stay away! Plague, there's plague here —"

Sheppard said something under his breath, and slung his weapon on his chest again. "It's all right. We've come to help."

He started toward the — it was a child, Blaze realized, a skinny child in a grubby shirt and not much more, but at that age he couldn't tell if it were male or female — and the child took three skipping steps backward, waving the banner again.

"No, stay back! You'll catch your deaths!"

Sheppard stopped. "We're from Atlantis, we've come to help you."

"You brought the Wraith," the child answered, and Blaze heard Everlasting hiss behind him.

"They're — well, it's a long story, but we won't let them hurt you," Sheppard said.

"If there are people here who are sick, we can help them," the Young Queen said. "We have medicines with us, and can bring more."

The child made a small sound like a sob, but shook its head wildly. "Grandmother says, no one is to come in. Otherwise they'll catch it and die."

Sheppard went to one knee. "So your — grandmother? She told you to keep watch, keep people out? That's very brave of you."

"If you go in, you'll die." The child sniffled. "Everybody's going to die."

"Not if you let us help you," Sheppard said. "I bet I can guess what's wrong — the blood fever, right? We've got medicine for that, and we can help you. If you'll let us."

The child hesitated. "We don't have any money."

"We don't need to be paid," the Young Queen said. "Once we have treated your people, if any are well enough to answer a few questions — that would be helpful to us. But first let us help."

A figure appeared in the doorway of the largest building, an old woman in a long dress and a filthy apron, a strip of once-bright fabric wrapped around her hair.

"Bina! Tell them to go!"

The child darted back to her, the scarlet flag flying behind it, bright against the yellowing grass. "Granny, they've come to help!"

"No!" The old woman caught the child by the shoulders, turned it firmly away from the door. "Stay out, Bina, you know you must. Strangers, the blood fever has us. Run, before it takes you, too!"

"We have come from Atlantis," the Young Queen said, taking a couple of careful steps forward. "I am Teyla Emmagen, once of Athos and now of Atlantis. We were called here to help treat this plague. We can help you if you'll let us."

"Atlantis?" The old woman swayed, and caught herself against the door's frame. "Truly? From Atlantis?"

"Yes." The Young Queen nodded firmly. "Let us help you."

"No one can help us," the old woman said, but she did not offer further protest as the Young Queen came closer.

Sheppard bit his lip, looking from the houses to the Marines and then the jumper. "Ok. Ronon, you and Hernandez stay with the Wraith, keep them out of our way. McKay, contact Dr. Beckett and tell him we need another med team here as quickly as possible. We'll get them more information in flight, but assume we've got a village full of sick people."

"Right," McKay answered, and bustled away.

"The rest of you, come with me." Sheppard turned

without waiting for an answer, and the Marines followed.

After a moment, Salt laughed softly. "And now we simply wait?"

"Yes." Ronon's thumb caressed the butt of his weapon.

"What of our queen?" Blaze asked.

Ronon shrugged. "Looks like she caused the epidemic. I doubt you'll find her alive."

"All the more reason for us to make haste," Blaze snapped. And the crash itself had been bad, bad enough to kill even if there had been no sickness.

"Nope." Ronon shook his head. "You heard Sheppard. We wait here until help comes."

Blaze drew breath to protest, his claws flexing, and Forge laid a hand on his sleeve.

Wait. I do not think your queen has been here. The child was not afraid.

Everlasting lifted his head. *True. If there had been a Culling — if any of us had hunted here —*

Forge nodded. *The child would not have been so calm. And if Moonwhite did not come here, then she was not exposed to the fever.*

That was true, though the consequences of that wreck might be bad enough. Blaze took a deep breath and then another, forcing himself to remain calm. He could not make the Lanteans do his will — they were, like it or not, entirely at the humans' mercy in this. But he would put up with it if it meant finding his queen.

Even though the Lanteans were clearly making all possible haste, it was another hour before the second jumper arrived with Dr. Beckett and his team. They vanished into the largest building, lugging boxes and equipment with them, and after a while Sheppard and the Young Queen emerged together, the Young Queen rehanging her weapon. Forge felt the others' attention sharpen, fear ready to change to anger, and stepped quickly forward.

"What news?"

"There were about forty people in this village," Sheppard said. "Maybe half of them are still alive, and maybe Beckett can pull them through."

"And it is the blood fever?" Forge didn't look back, but cast his thought in that direction. *Let me see what they know before we make demands.*

He felt reluctant agreement from Blaze and Everlasting, and something like approval from Salt. The Young Queen nodded. "Unmistakably so."

"And there is no sign that our queen has been there," Forge said "or you would have said so already."

"That is also true," the Young Queen said, serenely.

"At least no one left alive knows about any Wraith attack," Sheppard said. "Now, it seems to me that your queen might have sneaked up and grabbed a snack, and no one who knew about it has survived…"

"If that were so, you would have found the body," Forge said. "And I do not believe you didn't look."

Sheppard grinned. "As it happens, we did. And, no, we didn't find anyone who'd been sucked dry. Now whether that's good news or bad news — you tell me."

Forge tipped his head to one side, considering. "I would call it good news. And also evidence that we did not cause this plague. If illness had caused the crash, our queen and any other survivors would have come here to feed and restore themselves, and, yes, transmission between Wraith and human is always possible, though to be avoided for obvious reasons. But if they did not come here — either they are dead in the wreck, which is still possible, or they went elsewhere, and we must find them."

The brief amusement drained from Sheppard's face. "Yeah. Back to the ship."

It was a long walk back to the site of the wreck, through a scrubby forest that smelled sharply of resin. They were higher than Forge had realized at first, and he felt his lungs labor from the altitude as they climbed the first slope, until his body adjusted to the new conditions. He glanced at the others, and Blaze gave him a wry smile.

We will adapt.

Have adapted, Everlasting corrected, without heat, and Forge felt Blaze's pulse of amusement. He had forgotten how much he had once liked Moonwhite's consort, when they had all been young together on Edge's hive. Salt smiled as though he'd caught the thought, and Forge glanced at him.

And you? Are you well?

I am old, not decayed, Salt answered, and Forge felt the blood rise in his cheeks.

No offense was meant.

And none taken, Salt said, with just enough surprise that Forge thought he was sincere. He paused, lifting his head to test the air. *We are close, I think.*

Forge took a deep breath, and grimaced at the taste

of shell and metal and dead flesh. *Yes —*

"There," Everlasting said aloud, and pointed.

Ahead, several of the trees had been snapped in half, the jagged ends of the broken trunks still weeping beads of sap, and a tangle of tree tops lay across their path. They climbed cautiously around the mess, and emerged into another, smaller clearing that ended abruptly in a barren slope so steep as to be very nearly a cliff. The scout was crumpled against it, the right forward quadrant crushed into the rising ground. The hull was torn open on that side, and along the belly, and trails of fluid ran from the broken skin to puddle unpleasantly in the mud.

The hatch is open, Blaze said, incandescent relief in his tone, and started forward.

"Hang on," Sheppard said, and the Marines cocked their weapons, the sound loud in the still air.

"The hatch," Blaze repeated aloud. "Someone survived."

"Yeah, but are they friendly?" Sheppard gave his uneasy smile.

"Quite possibly not," Forge said, and put himself between Blaze and the ship. "But if there is anyone alive aboard, they will be more friendly to us than to you. And if one of our kin is wounded, they are likely to feed first and ask questions later."

"That is true," the Young Queen said, with a glance at Sheppard, and Ronon shook his head.

"One of us should go with them."

Sheppard bit his lip. "You —" He pointed to Salt. "You stay here. Ronon, Casey, go with the rest of them."

"That is fair," Forge said, fixing his eyes on Blaze, and the consort nodded reluctantly.

Very well.

Blaze led the way into the broken hull, Everlasting on his heels, and Forge followed more slowly. The humans came behind them, muttering at the darkness, and there was a flash as they switched on lights. Everlasting gave them an annoyed glance, but Blaze caught his sleeve.

Forward first.

Yes, Everlasting agreed, and they made their way deeper into the broken hull.

The scout was small, designed for speed over short distances, and the living quarters were merely adequate, narrow chambers not distinguished by any special markings. Even the one that must have been intended for the queen was bare and plain, only the larger nest and the broken coils of what had been a fountain to mark it as special.

There are no goods here, Everlasting said. *No belongings.*

She would not have brought much, Blaze answered, his tone bleak. *It means nothing.*

Forge opened the single storage unit nonetheless, and found it empty, with no sign that it had ever contained anything.

It means nothing, Blaze said again, and led them further along the central corridor.

The damage was worse as they approached the control room, and the air smelled of smoke and death. Forge bared his teeth unhappily, and behind him he heard the Marine break out in a fit of coughing.

"What died?" Ronon demanded, and Forge glanced over his shoulder.

"The ship is dead." He grimaced as another scent struck him. "But also —"

"The pilot is dead," Blaze said, from the entrance to the control room. The touch of his mind was bleak as he continued. *Flame — my brother that I brought with me to my queen's hive.*

Everlasting hissed softly, and pulled the other blade gently aside. Forge slipped past them both to enter the control room, stepping carefully over broken floor plates and exposed conduit, shattered screens and consoles that bore the marks of fire. The pilot, Flame, had fallen forward at his post, lay draped over the controls, his hair clotted with blood. The smell of death was strong, but Forge mastered himself enough to touch the corpse, feeling for the life-points. Flame had been dead for some days — killed in the crash, from the wound that caved in his high forehead. Forge winced, and wiped his hands on the skirts of his long coat. There was no sign of Moonwhite or any other of her men.

What can you find? Everlasting asked from the door.

Forge turned slowly, looking for an undamaged console. The navigation station was least touched, its screen merely cracked rather than destroyed, and he ran his hands along the edge of the console, feeling for any residual power. There was none: if any part of *Nimble* had survived the crash, it hadn't lasted long. He reached into the pockets of his coat and found an emergency power cell, fitted it into the clips beneath the console. The screen flickered weakly, displayed a cascade of symbols, and froze.

The main computer is dead, he said, scanning the symbols that were already beginning to fade. *This is the crash data — there was some emergency, they were looking for a landing site, and this was the first they found.*

What caused the emergency, can you tell? Blaze pushed past Everlasting, and came to join him, wincing as he saw the extent of his brother's injuries. *Was there a problem with the ship?*

I can't tell, Forge answered, and looked around again. There were no other undamaged consoles, and he reached into his coat for a cleverman's handheld scanner, found a cord and patched it into the console that had once controlled *Nimble's* internal systems. It beeped a warning, and displayed a confused hash of symbols: if anything was wrong, it had been in the environmental systems, but the readings were inconclusive. Or… He frowned, and moved to the commander's station. It was unmarked, though the small screens were dead, unmarred by either damage or blood. If Moonwhite had been sitting there, it was good odds she had survived the crash. He tried the scanner again, but there was no power in this section, and there was no way to provide any, at least not with the tools he had at hand. *I'm not seeing any signs of major damage. There was possibly a problem with the environmentals, but even that is unclear.*

Contagion? Blaze's tone was sharp with fear.

Forge drew a slow breath. *It is possible. I can't say for sure.*

"Hey." Ronon leaned down to peer through the hatch. "If you haven't found anything, let's get out of here."

"I am not yet finished," Forge said. He looked around again. Every scout was subtly different, each ship grown from its own seed to take unique form; they all contained the same systems, but the points of access were always different. There, he thought, that was the port for the secondary computer, and for a mercy it wasn't as badly damaged as some of the other consoles. No power, though, and he removed the emergency cell from the navigation console and clipped it into place. The screen sparked, and he hastily plugged in his scanner, diverting the data to its screen. The symbols scrolled past, and he hissed in spite of himself.

Well? Blaze demanded.

This indicates that they had sickness aboard, though not what kind. Forge scrolled back through the data. *If it were blood fever, I would expect them to say so.*

They cannot have infected the humans here, Everlasting said. *There's no indication that they had any contact with that village, or with any other.*

But she is alive, Blaze said. *Or she was when they landed. Otherwise we would have found her body.*

I believe so, Forge said. Though whether she had been injured, or if she were sick enough — there was no guarantee that she still survived.

"Are you finished?" Ronon demanded again, and this time Forge nodded.

"We are done. The queen is not here."

"So where is she?" Ronon gestured for them to precede him down the corridor, and Forge obeyed, the others trailing behind him.

"I don't know."

"She survived the crash," Blaze said. "We must find her."

CHAPTER THREE

SALT LIFTED his head as the rest of his party emerged from the wreck, the humans still behind them with weapons ready. The Young Queen turned, her expression one of curiosity, and Sheppard lifted his head.

"Anything?" he called, and the big Satedan shook his head.

"One dead Wraith. Killed in the crash."

"We believe that our queen survived," Blaze said. His voice was steady, but Salt could feel the banked worry beneath it. "And possibly some of her men. But they could not stay here."

"Why not?" McKay asked. He waved vaguely at the wreck. "There's shelter, ok, it smells bad, but it's better than being out in the open."

"Our ships are living things," Forge said, with what Salt felt was commendable patience. "Certain parts will decompose."

"I've been on downed Wraith ships that were intact," Sheppard said.

"I said certain parts," Forge answered. "Once they have rotted — or once they are destroyed, that is also always possible — then the wreck will serve. But not until then."

"Why do you think your queen survived?" the Young Queen asked, and Salt felt another flare of fear from Blaze, but his answer was calm enough.

"As your man said, we found a single body, that of the pilot. We did not find our queen, nor any of the other blades who accompanied her. I believe she left the wreck."

"Why?" McKay asked. "I mean, yes, ok, to get away from the ship while it decomposed, but presumably she was looking for something, right?"

"I'm more interested in why the ship crashed," Sheppard said. "And why it crashed here."

"We don't know," Forge said. For an instant, he looked drained and ill, then composed himself with an effort. "It seems possible that there was illness on board, and that they sought to feed and heal themselves, but I can't be sure. The ship's records are destroyed, and I was only able to salvage a very little."

"Which makes you responsible for the epidemic," Ronon said.

"It does not," Forge said, his voice sharp. "There is still no sign that the queen or any of her blades went into that village, no sign that she, they, fed there. Her consort is right, we need to search for her immediately."

"If it wasn't you, how did the fever spread?" Sheppard demanded.

"There is no proof that it has," Forge said. "The crash and the sickness could be entirely unrelated — even if there was illness aboard our scout, I cannot say what it was, or whether it affected more than the ship itself. And I repeat what I have said before: there is no sign that our queen or her men ever entered the village." He paused, his expression thoughtful. "If I were pressed — the scout must have been seen entering the atmosphere, and the crash would have been heard. Perhaps one of the villagers came to investigate, and brought the fever back with them. If it is the same illness."

"Nobody said anything about a crash," Sheppard said. "Or about finding any dead Wraith."

"They were pretty sick," McKay said. "I hate to say it, Sheppard, but if one of them did bring back the virus, there might not be anyone there who'd remember, never mind being well enough to tell us."

"This is all speculation," the Young Queen said. "Where would your queen go, if not to the village to feed?"

Forge showed his off hand, palm out and open. "I can't say."

"She might have sought shelter elsewhere," Blaze said. "Shelter and a way to contact the hive. If she was not injured, she would not need to feed —"

"What if she was sick?" Ronon asked.

"We are strong." Blaze glared at him. "She might well choose to fight the infection rather than risk contaminating our food supply."

"They're not your food supply," Ronon snapped.

"Ronon's got a point," Sheppard said, his hands loose on the weapon strapped to his chest. "This planet is on our side of the line."

"A line to which we have not yet agreed," Everlasting snarled.

"So why should we believe you about anything?" Ronon's smile was ugly.

"Colonel," the Young Queen said. "The best way to answer all these questions is to find their queen."

There was a moment of silence, and then, slowly, the Lanteans relaxed. Sheppard nodded sharply, and Ronon took his thumb off the controls of his weapon. McKay said, "So, if she didn't stay here, and she didn't go into the village — up into the hills?"

Salt eyed the slope unhappily. "Not here, I don't think."

"Sir, there's a break further along," one of the Marines — Hernandez, the others had called him — said. "Looks like somebody could get up there pretty easily."

Sheppard looked at Blaze. "Well?"

The Consort sighed. "Let us begin there." He turned in the direction that Hernandez had indicated, and the others fell into step beside him. The Lanteans followed as well, their weapons ready.

Salt made no great effort to keep up, content to let the younger and more skilled take the lead. As Hernandez had said, the cliff ended only a little way beyond the edge of the clearing where *Nimble* had crashed, becoming a slope of tumbled rocks and then a shallower incline studded with stunted trees, their limbs twisted by winter winds. Blaze paused to scan the area, and Everlasting stooped with an exclamation.

Here!

Blaze bent to see, and Salt lengthened his stride to join them. *What have you found?*

Footprints, Everlasting said. He looked from the scuffed earth to the top of the slope as though measuring distance. *I think they went that way.*

Salt looked at the mark, unable to tell it from any other, and Sheppard said, "Ok, what have you got?"

"I believe they went over the ridge," Everlasting said, and turned without waiting for an answer.

Salt concealed a grimace and followed dutifully. He was getting old for this sort of chase, and had never been good at it even when he was young. The Lanteans followed, too, careful to stay out of reach and to keep their weapons ready. At the top of the ridge, Everlasting gave another cry.

"Here. They have left us a trail."

So she was alive and well, Blaze said. Everlasting and Forge exchanged wary glances, but neither of them had the heart to say what they were clearly thinking. And no more do I, Salt thought, because I'm sure Blaze knows it well enough. Moonwhite was alive and well then, but that promised nothing for the future.

The ridge dropped to a narrow valley, the ground rising more steeply on its far side. The blades cast about, and found a second mark halfway up the shorter slope. It ended in a spreading meadow, short wiry grass starred with thousands of tiny yellow flowers that ran gently uphill to another upthrust slab of rock. The air was chill here, and growing scant of oxygen. Salt paused, letting his lungs adjust, and heard the other Marine, Casey, break out in a coughing fit, his hands on his knees.

"You ok?" Sheppard asked, and the man nodded.

"Fine, sir."

Blaze and Everlasting conferred briefly and then turned in opposite directions, scanning the ground for another mark. Forge stood open-mouthed, breathing hard to force his lungs to change again, and at Salt's side the Young Queen said, "You are not like the others."

Salt started. She moved as quietly as the children of Osprey; he had not felt her approach, and he had to take a quick breath to let his heart slow before he could answer. "I'm not sure what you mean."

"You are not a warrior — a blade? — or a scientist like Forge."

"That is so," he said, cautiously.

"Then what is your function?"

He hesitated, but could see no harm in answering. "I am — I make stories. I weave memories for the hives."

"A historian?" The Young Queen tilted her head to one side, her expression, he thought, genuinely curious.

Salt considered in turn. "In part? But not all my stories are true, many are pure invention."

Her eyebrows rose. "Ah. I did not know there were such among the Wraith."

"We — it is not a common talent," Salt said, and wondered why he boasted to this human. "I have practiced my craft for many years, and am well thought of among the hives where I am known."

"So you do not belong to any particular hive," the Young Queen said.

He paused again, but could see no way the information could help her. "In the old days, storymakers traveled freely among the hives. All queens held their hands over us, and we were not part of any feud, however sisterly, and no matter what our lineage was. In later years, I spent much of my time on the hive of Moonwhite's mother, and was counted among her favorites."

"Which means you knew this missing queen when she was a child," the Young Queen said.

"I did." Salt bent his head again.

"Is that why you came?"

Before Salt could decide how to answer that,

Everlasting called from the middle of the meadow. "Here! Another marker."

Salt moved toward him, the Young Queen at his side, to see Everlasting pointing to a pile of stones. A flat slab had been broken into thirds and the parts piled on top of each other, and a directional symbol had been cut into the uppermost surface. The lines were jagged and uneven: was it just the difficulty of using the tool for an unfamiliar purpose, or did that betray sickness and failing strength?

That triggered a memory, faint and wavering, and Salt stopped, closing his eyes as he tried to focus on the image. Many years ago, so many years ago — Edge had been alive then, but he had not been with her hive, she had sent him to amuse a sister queen of Night with whom she sought an alliance. And there Salt had heard a tale, a queen healed seemingly by magic, and when he doubted, Twilight Shadow had sent him with one of her clevermen to see the place where it had happened.

"This way," Blaze said aloud. *Among those trees.*

Trees that stood stripped of all but a few leaves, their branches bare and twisted, their outlines oddly blurred.

Stop! Salt caught Blaze's arm, pulling him to a stop. "Stop, no one move."

He heard the clicks as the Marines cocked their weapons, and Sheppard said, with a creditable assumption of annoyance, "What the hell?"

"This is iratus country," Salt said. "Those trees are webbed for their hunting."

"No, no, no, no, no," McKay said. "We're not going to deal with any of those things again."

"Tell me you're kidding me." Sheppard was looking profoundly unhappy.

Salt cocked his head. "Why would I joke?"

"Never mind." Sheppard shook his head. "You're telling me there's an iratus colony somewhere nearby."

"I think so," Salt said.

It makes sense, Forge began, then shook his head and repeated the words aloud. "If she were desperate — the bite of an iratus queen can cure many diseases."

"I didn't think that was exactly guaranteed," Sheppard said.

Forge gave Blaze an apologetic glance. "It is an act of last resort, yes, and it is not always successful. But if she had fed recently —"

"You said she didn't attack the village," Ronon pointed out.

Everlasting bared teeth at him. "Every man of hers would be proud to give his life."

"So you're saying she just ate her people," Ronon said.

"We don't know," Forge said firmly, overriding both Blaze and Sheppard. "But if she was ill, and there are iratus here, it would explain why she chose this path."

"I don't intend for any of us to get anywhere near an iratus nest," Sheppard said. "That's not happening."

"If our queen is there," Blaze said, "she will need our help."

"Did you hear what I said?" Sheppard asked. "We're not getting near them."

Salt took a careful breath. "No one wants to risk their attack, not even Wraith. But — I am a storymaker. I can..." He shook his head, unable to find a word that matched the exercise of his art. "I can subdue them, keep them still and harmless. We must try."

"We will stand between you and the nest," Forge said. "Wraith are somewhat less vulnerable to their bite."

"We cannot leave the queen unaccounted for," the Young Queen said.

Sheppard sighed. "All right. We'll look for the nest, and see if your queen is there. If she is — we'll see. But in the meantime, everybody stays well back from those things."

"Yes," Everlasting said, and Salt nodded.

"That is all we can ask."

Everlasting studied the fine sheets of webbing that hung between the bare trees. It was an iratus web, all right, the fine, almost invisible sheets that they spun when hunting. At each corner, and twice more at seemingly random points, the silk was thicker and twisted into a nub; he shifted to his left and caught the tell-tale glint of messenger threads running into the underbrush.

There.

I see them, Blaze answered, moving carefully to the right. *And — yes, two more heading into the rocks.*

Everlasting looked where the other consort indicated, and followed the messenger into a shadowed crevice. He hissed softly. *I'd guess the hunter was there.*

There might be another under the leaves, Blaze answered.

Everlasting nodded. *Maybe.* He shifted again, trying to follow the path of the gossamer strands. *How do you want to take them?*

If we destroy the trap, we'll bring the nest out to see what's happened, Blaze said, *but I don't see another way around. Unless we went over the slope, above the hunter?*

Everlasting considered, the thrill of the hunt rising in his blood. It had been a long time since he'd last hunted anything — their last Cullings had been unopposed, chasing screaming humans into the Darts' culling beams, hardly a challenge, never mind sport. *Yes. And if you went that way, you could collapse that crevice as you passed.*

I? Blaze's amusement flickered over him, and Everlasting smiled.

Unless you would prefer to deal with the one in the leaves.

All of which will still bring out the nest if you make a mistake, Forge said. *Unless Salt can weave them to stillness from a distance?*

The storymaker shook his head. *I can only act on those I see.*

"Hey, how about an update?" Sheppard asked, and Everlasting damped down his enjoyment.

"We are working out the best way to pass this trap."

"What about just going around it?" Ronon asked.

"There will be four or five watchers in this web,* Everlasting answered. "If we can kill them, there's a chance we won't bring the entire nest out even if we disturb the web. And there will be more webs closer to the nest."

"Lovely," Sheppard muttered.

There is something odd here, Salt said. *These webs — the silk is old.*

Surely not, Blaze said, and Everlasting frowned. Everyone knew that iratus bugs renewed their webs with the day's dawn, mending tears and frayed edges when the rising sun would quickly harden the strands of silk. And yet... He moved closer, until he could almost touch the first thin sheet. Like the messenger threads, it was hard to see unless you found just the right angle, but when you did — Salt was right, there were long tears in the center of the sheet, as though the wind had caught it and the iratus had not yet repaired it. There had been no wind on their climb up the mountain. Only the messenger lines looked solid.

Salt is right, he said, and looked at the Young Queen. "There is something strange about this trap. The iratus have not maintained it."

"And what does that mean?" Sheppard asked.

Everlasting glanced at the others, and received only mental shrugs in answer. "We don't know."

"But you still think there's an active nest further up the hill," Sheppard said.

I think it's likely, Salt said, and Everlasting nodded. "Yes. And if our queen is there —"

We cannot leave her, Blaze said.

Forge laid a hand on his sleeve, urging caution. Everlasting went on, carefully, "We must find it, yes. But we must not rush in without precautions."

"What did you have in mind?" Sheppard asked.

Everlasting ignored him, studying the layout of the webs. The outermost sheet was the most damaged, as he would have expected, held together by the sturdier weave of the edges and the attachment points for the messenger lines. The central portion had split into four long panels, and when he blew on the nearest, the silk belled, but did not tear further. He fanned it with his off hand, creating a wind strong enough to move two of the messenger lines that led to the crevice, but nothing happened.

That is odd, Blaze said.

Very. Everlasting shifted his position, trying to reach another part of the web, and Ronon caught him by the shoulder.

"Hold on."

In the same moment, McKay said sharply, "What are you trying to do, get us all eaten?"

"There is something wrong with this web," Everlasting said. "I am not sure it is even watched —"

"What's wrong with it is that it's full of iratus bugs," Sheppard said.

"But I'm not sure it is," Everlasting said. "This web is torn, and so are the ones within. Iratus mend their webs every day. It's possible this is abandoned."

"But not for very long," the Young Queen said.

Everlasting dipped his head in agreement. "No, not long."

So — nothing in the crevice? Blaze asked, then shook his head and repeated the words aloud.

"I don't think so." Everlasting looked at Ronon. "Take your hand off me, and I will see if there are still hunters beneath the leaves."

"Sheppard?" Ronon didn't move, and Sheppard bit his lip.

"Yeah, let him try. Casey, if any bugs come out — shoot them."

Is that a good idea? Forge asked, and Everlasting shrugged.

It should kill them. If there are any there. Ronon released him, and he moved further along the line of the web, angling himself so that he was able to reach the section where the messenger lines led beneath the leaves. He blew on it first, and got no reaction, then waved his hand. This time, the messenger moved enough to disturb the leaves, and there was an answering movement from beneath.

"Look out!" McKay exclaimed, and in the same moment a pair of iratus bugs emerged from under the leaves, forelegs probing the soft ground.

Casey and Sheppard brought up their weapons at the same moment, and fired a long burst into the leaves. The bugs disintegrated under the hail of bullets, leaving nothing but a few fragments of carapace on the churned ground.

"Oh, that's nice," McKay said, in the sudden silence.

"Rodney," the Young Queen said.

"Well, really, that's like taking high explosive to a spider —"

"They were slow," Salt said. "Too slow."

Everlasting nodded, scanning the hill above the webs. There was no sign of further reaction, nothing to indicate that they had disturbed the nest, or even that the nest was reacting at all to the death of two of its drones. "They should have responded by now. If they are going to."

If the queen is in the hive — if the iratus queen is concentrating on her, Forge said, *the others should be absorbed by that as well.*

You're sure of that? Blaze demanded.

No, Forge answered. *No, I'm not. But that's my best guess.* He shaded his eyes to peer up the hill. *There's another web there, between those two low trees, and I think another one beyond it.*

Sheppard cleared his throat. "Ok, we've killed two iratus bugs —"

"Out of what are probably thousands in a nest," McKay interjected. "What? You think I'm underestimating how really disturbing this is likely to be?"

"I'd say this was about the last word in disturbing," Sheppard answered, "but we don't have a lot of choice." He looked at Everlasting. "What's your plan?"

"The nest is likely to be in a cave above us," Everlasting said, scanning the slope. "If Forge is right, and the iratus are occupied queen to queen, it is possible that we can go around the sentry webs — this one, and those up there." He pointed to a scrape of bare rock. "If we climb that, I think we will be able to see the nest."

Sheppard bit his lip again. "You're not even sure the nest is up there."

"There is certainly a nest," Everlasting answered. "But, no, I don't know exactly where it is, nor will we until we climb higher."

"Ok." Sheppard took a breath. "Hernandez, you and I will go with the Wraith. Ronon, McKay, Teyla, Casey. You'll stay here. If anything goes wrong, pile in with full firepower."

"I believe I should accompany you," the Young Queen said, but Sheppard met her stare squarely.

"You can keep an eye on things from down here, can't

you? I don't want to take any more people up there than absolutely necessary."

There was a moment of silence, and then she nodded. "I can do so, though not, of course, as well. As you wish."

Sheppard nodded. "All right. So we go around these webs, and up that rock, and then?"

"Then we will see," Everlasting answered. He didn't dare look at Blaze, who looked grimmer than ever. If it were his own queen, if Light Breaking lay at death's door, hostage to the legendary powers of an iratus queen — no, he couldn't bear the idea any more than Blaze could. He gathered the other Wraith with a glance. "Let's go."

They made their way cautiously up the slope, skirting the webs and the remains of the two iratus bugs, and then scrambling awkwardly up the steep slab of rock that jutted out of the ground, showing bands of dark stone in a pale matrix. It led to another, and then a broader, less tilted stretch, and Everlasting lifted his hand in warning. Blaze stopped instantly, a step behind and two arms-lengths to his left. The others, Forge and Salt and the two humans, straggled to a halt behind them. Above them, the slope evened out enough that a handful of stunted trees clung to the slope, their branches clogged with shreds of silk, and beyond them a shadowed opening led into the hill. A boot protruded from beneath the nearest tree, the familiar black shape of a blade's gear. Blaze hissed at the sight, and Everlasting lifted his hand again.

Wait. We must consider our approach.

He felt Blaze's agreement like banked fire. *Below the

trees. There are no webs there.*

And also our line of escape should the nest swarm, Everlasting said, as though the other hadn't answered.

Below him, Salt stirred. *I believe I can hold them. I can feel them now.*

And our queen? Blaze's tone was sharply afraid.

No.

Which means nothing, Everlasting said. He looked over his shoulder at the waiting humans. "We must get closer."

Sheppard gave a short nod. "I'm seeing a body up there."

"So do we all." Everlasting considered the slope, shaping a mental picture for the others: to reach the cave, skirt the edge of the stones, being careful not to slip down into the webs that filmed the shrubs at its lower edge.

I will try to reach the injured, Forge said, and Everlasting nodded.

Salt will weave the hive to stasis if he can, and then we will see what we find. If we rouse the nest… He pictured their best escape route, across bare stone and along the curve of the hill. It was not ideal, the footing poor and the line steep, but surely the Lanteans' weapons would hold back the iratus long enough to make good their escape.

Let's hope it doesn't come to that, Forge muttered.

Everlasting ignored him, and spoke aloud, wishing that there were some easier way to convey his plan to the humans. "We will track along the edge of the rock until we can see the cave, and Salt will — stun them. If anything goes wrong, we will retreat the way we came, and then back along this ridge. If you cover us with your weapons, there is a chance we will all get away."

"You're not making me feel real good about those odds," Sheppard said.

"It's the hunt we have," Everlasting answered, and to his surprise the Lantean gave a wry grin.

"Yeah. Do me a favor and don't upset those things, ok?"

"We will do our best," Everlasting answered, and started up the slope.

He took his time on the approach, stopping often to check for the fine-spun bands of webbing that the iratus used to warn the nest of intruders. Twice they had to work their way around those traps, stepping carefully from stone to stone, but at last they topped the band of stone and could see the cave clearly. It was an iratus nest, all right, sheets of webbing blanketing the entrance, and the thin veils did nothing to hide the heavy shape of egg sacs suspended from the ceiling. Three blades lay beneath the trees, shriveled to husks; a fourth lay closer to the entrance, his eyes closed and his features sharp with injury. His coat was ripped in a dozen places, but from the look of things, he had begun to heal.

Blaze's expression was taut with fear. *Moonwhite.*

It was barely the breath of a thought, but Everlasting caught the other consort by the arm.

Let Salt work.

The storymaker moved to his left along the edge of the level area, testing his footing as he went. Satisfied, he faced the cave opening and held out both hands, palms up, the familiar gesture of a maker beginning his tale. Everlasting felt mist rise, a common prologue, but instead of the clean scent of water, it was filled with the taste of resin, the heavy smoke of burning athorn. There was an answering hum from the nest, a stirring as though all the iratus rubbed carapace against carapace, and Everlasting braced himself to flee. Blaze caught his breath, and Everlasting heard the sharp clicking as the Lanteans readied their weapons. There was a rustle from the leaves beside the injured blade, a ripple of movement that might have been an iratus bug moving to attack. Everlasting braced himself to leap and grab — they had no other weapons that would be effective, and the wounded man was in the Lanteans' line of fire — but there was no further movement.

Softly, Forge said, his thought a mere thread among the smoke, as though he hadn't meant to speak at all.

Salt did not move, the smoke thickening around them, and slowly the sound subsided. Blaze drew breath, every muscle tensing, and then subsided. Everlasting admired his control. The illusion of resin was stronger, the air darkening as though it were the day's end; the quality of the light was like water dragging at his limbs, lulling him toward sleep.

See if that one is quiescent, Salt said, to Forge, and the cleverman moved cautiously toward the source of that nearby rustle. After a moment's search, he found a long stick, and used it to flip back the blanket of leaves. An iratus lay revealed, black carapace gleaming, six clawed legs and the long clawed tail, but it did not move.

"Kill it," Sheppard said, from down the slope.

Forge flinched, but the iratus did not move. *With

what?* he began, and switched to speech. "I cannot. I must retrieve this one."

As he spoke, he stooped to take the unconscious blade by the shoulders, and heaved him back onto the bare rock. Everlasting could see that the front of the blade's coat and the shirt beneath it were both cut to ribbons, revealing patches of newly healed skin. Forge laid his feeding hand against the blade's throat, testing warily.

He will revive soon, but he will need to feed.

That was no surprise: to have healed those injuries would have taken most of his strength. *Keep him away from the Lanteans, then,* Everlasting said, and felt the prick of Forge's amusement.

Our queen, Blaze said again.

Give me just a moment longer, Salt said. His thought was as languid as his illusion, barely distinguishable from the urge to rest, to give in to the coming night. Night, and winter, too, Everlasting thought, dragging himself out of the spell. The mist had taken on an edge of ice, of long nights under a flickering sky: Wraith and iratus alike felt the pull of hibernation, heartbeat slowing, the blood retreating from fingers and toes. Everlasting gave a silent snarl and shook himself, deliberately rejecting the illusion, and focused on the bodies by the door. All were blades, presumably all part of Moonwhite's crew, and — though he thought the one on the bottom of the pile bore the mark of an iratus bite — all were drained, dead at another Wraith's hand. The queen herself, probably, drawing on their strength to keep herself alive long enough to enter the nest alive, which meant she had been desperate indeed... He saw the same thought, the same fear, in Blaze's face, and made himself project more confidence than he felt.

She reached here alive. We will find her in the cave.

He felt the flicker of doubt, of fear, and Blaze turned his attention to Salt. *Well?*

The storymaker's eyes were closed, and his out-stretched hands had begun to tremble, but the illusion was still strong around them. *Try and see.*

That was not as reassuring an answer as Everlasting had hoped for. He slew that thought, and considered the opening. The iratus were silent, stunned by Salt's illusion, but he could still see nothing beyond the first layer of webbing. *We'll have to get closer.*

Yes. Blaze took a step forward and then another, careful to step only on bare ground.

"Be ready," Everlasting said aloud, to the waiting Lanteans, and followed Blaze. Two steps and a pause, then another step, then three, and at last they were at the edge of the opening, close enough at last to see through the draped webs. More egg sacs hung from the ceiling, enormous ovoids half as tall as a blade, and three times as wide: the hive was preparing to spawn. A few iratus clung to the sides or dangled from the cords that held the sacs to the ceiling, but most of them were on the cave floor, gathered in clumps and piles as the illusion triggered the instinct to hibernate. Further in, past the first webs, where the stones rose slightly, there was a humped shape that resolved as he stared harder to a queen lying half on her side, half on her back, her Night-black hair in tangles around her as though she had fallen haphazard, rather than laid herself down to await healing or death. An iratus queen clung to her chest like a sinister jewel, its scarlet belly pulsing softly.

Moonwhite, Blaze whispered again, and Everlasting winced at his pain.

The webs that covered the opening were as tattered as the ones they had seen further down the slope, and there were fewer messenger lines. Everlasting let the knife he carried in his sleeve slide down into his hand. *If we remove the center of the web, the messengers will remain untouched.*

Blaze nodded. *We can reach the queen, I see a path.*

Everlasting brought the knife to his lips, breathed on it to fog the surface so that the traces of moisture would help the metal pass through the clinging silk. He made one cut, withdrawing the knife as soon as he felt the silk begin to pull, and froze as several of the iratus rattled softly. He was close enough that he could see the plates of their carapaces shifting, chiton whispering against chiton — close enough that it would be hard enough to fend off even one, never mind six or seven. He felt the illusion strengthen, a gust of imaginary snow wafting across the opening, and the iratus stilled again.

He breathed on the knife again, cut another swath — the iratus were quiet this time — and then another, until there was a gap large enough for a blade to slip through. He slid the knife back into his sleeve, and Blaze shook his head.

I'll go.

She was his queen; it was his right. Everlasting dipped his head, agreement and acknowledgement, wishing he had better weapons to hand. If the iratus woke, there was little he could do with only a pair of knives — give Blaze a clean death, perhaps, but even that was hardly guaranteed.

Go.

Blaze bent and slipped sideways through the gap in the web. The corners quivered, the messenger lines trembling, but the iratus did not move, held by Salt's vision. Blaze stepped between the next pair of webs, ducking beneath one of the hanging sacs, then threaded his way through the piles of iratus until he was within reach of Moonwhite's body. The other iratus had withdrawn from their queen, leaving a narrow cleared circle around the linked bodies, and Blaze stooped, gathering Moonwhite into his arms. The iratus queen's legs twitched, drawing new blood, dark against Moonwhite's skin, and there was another soft sussurent murmur from the iratus around her. Blaze froze, Moonwhite balanced awkwardly against his chest, and the iratus subsided again.

Blaze picked his way between the webs again, dodging the egg sacs, and came to a halt in front of the slit-open web. *You'll need to take her.*

Everlasting could feel Blaze's reluctance. He was no more eager himself, though for different reasons. If the iratus queen were jogged awake, if she turned on him... He pushed that thought away, and reached carefully through the web, using his elbows to spread the opening as wide as possible. Blaze laid her in his arms, and Everlasting braced himself to take her weight. She was utterly limp, and in spite of his best efforts, the iratus queen stirred again, carapace flaring. Fresh blood trickled from the wounds in Moonwhite's neck.

Easy, Blaze said, and Everlasting suppressed the urge to snarl at him. The iratus queen was practically against his chest, its scarlet belly pulsing slowly as it resettled itself on Moonwhite. Her face was starting to show the sharpness that went with hunger and injury: she, too, would need to feed once they had freed her from the iratus queen. At least Salt seemed to have it well under control, caught in his illusion of winter and fog and sleep. He turned his shoulders as Blaze held the web open and carefully drew Moonwhite out with him, back through the web and into the open space in front of the nest. Blaze followed, and in spite of his care, the web shivered and the iratus rustled again.

Outside, Salt stood like a stone, but his hands were shaking visibly now. Forge had dragged the surviving blade into a sitting position, but his eyes were still closed, the lids barely fluttering. They needed to get away before Salt lost control — needed to free Moonwhite from the thing still clamped to her neck.

I'll take her, Blaze said.

Everlasting started to object — surely it was better not to risk disturbing the iratus queen — but the fear and sorrow in Blaze's thought silenced him. He let Blaze take the queen's body, and turned to Salt. *How much longer?*

Not so very much, Salt answered, his voice slow, and in the nest more of the iratus stirred.

That answered one question, Everlasting thought. They would not be trying to remove the iratus queen here. *Go,* he said, to Forge and Blaze, and stooped himself to lift the injured blade. He was light with hunger, and it was less of a burden than he had feared to balance him over one shoulder. *Salt. Can you walk with me, and hold them just a little longer?*

I... There was a pause, long enough that Everlasting feared the worst, and then Salt nodded. *Yes. I can.*

Come with me, then.

Yes, Salt said again, and finally began to move, putting one foot in front of the other as though he walked in his sleep.

Everlasting picked his way down the slope, the strange blade balanced on his shoulder, following Blaze and Forge. Behind him, he could feel the illusion beginning to fray, and heard a scrape of stones as Salt stumbled and caught himself. The air was warmer, the mist fading; he quickened his step and saw the Lanteans falling back to the edge of the clearing as Blaze approached. He thought he heard a musing from the nest, and glanced over his shoulder to see Salt stumble again.

Focus on the queen, he said. *Keep her still, that will confuse the others —*

He felt Salt agree, and focused his own attention on the last stretch of ground. Surely there were no more iratus there, the Lanteans had killed them all, and he risked crossing the easier ground beside the damaged webs. Blaze laid Moonwhite gently on the ground, and Salt went to one knee beside her, his eyes closing as he concentrated on rebuilding his illusion.

"Shouldn't we be moving on?" McKay asked, looking past them up the hill. "I think I hear those things coming —"

Everlasting whipped around, but there was no sign of a swarm emerging from the nest. "We have crossed the edges of their territory," he said, with more confidence than he entirely felt. "Without the queen to goad them on, they will not pursue us."

"That's great," Sheppard said, from a safe distance, his hands ready on his weapon, "but how are you going to get that thing off her?"

Everlasting looked at Forge, who went to his knees beside Salt.

Can you persuade it to release her?

Salt showed teeth. *It's all I can do to keep it quiescent.*

"In our earlier encounter with the iratus bugs," the Young Queen said, "we were able to persuade it to release its victim by stopping the victim's heart."

"Except we don't have a defibrillator," McKay pointed out. "Not to mention that we don't know what a defibrillator would do to a Wraith anyway."

The Lanteans are right, Forge said. He laid his feeding hand carefully against Moonwhite's bared wrist, cocking his head as he tasted her condition. *And we cannot wait, both for Salt's sake and for hers.*

Everlasting let the blade he had been carrying slide to the ground. He knew what was required, though the risks were terrible — if they sapped Moonwhite's life too far, or did not restore it quickly enough, their attempt might well kill the queen. And if they didn't take enough, the iratus queen would keep its hold, and drain what was left of Moonwhite's life in an instant.

I can do it, Forge said, his tone reluctant, and Blaze shook his head.

No. That is my right, as consort. No one else shall touch her.

Fair enough. Everlasting dipped his head. *But wait a moment.* He switched to speech. "We are going to attempt to remove the queen, but I will need your help to incapacitate it. Do you have any of your smaller weapons?"

"What do you mean?" Sheppard asked.

"I think our safest choice is to shoot it as soon as it releases its claws," Everlasting said. "But not with those." He gestured to the weapon hanging from Sheppard's chest. "I have seen smaller weapons — pistols? If it is shot with that first, then it cannot attack, and we can knock it away so that it can be finished safely with those fast-fire weapons."

Sheppard nodded slowly. "Ok, yeah, I see what you're saying. Knock it out and then kill it. Except — can't he make it let go?"

"I cannot," Salt answered, not opening his eyes. "The iratus queen is too closely attached to her system."

"Damn." Sheppard gnawed at his underlip. "So you want — what? Me to put my pistol up against that thing and shoot it the minute it lets go?"

Everlasting nodded. "Or let me use your pistol, if you are unsure."

Sheppard gave a mirthless smile. "Yeah, no. I don't think so."

"Then you must do it," Everlasting said.

For an instant, he thought Sheppard would refuse, but then the human's mouth twisted, and he looked at the Young Queen. "Ok. Everybody off to the side. Casey, you'll do the honors once we get that thing loose." He turned back to Forge and Salt. "You'll have to give me room."

"Yes," Forge said, and rose gracefully to his feet. Salt backed away more slowly, and Sheppard went reluctantly to one knee, drawing his pistol and cocking it with a sharp sound that was echoed from among the Lanteans. Everlasting looked back sharply to see both Ronon and the second Marine with weapons leveled.

"We don't want you getting any ideas," the Satedan said.

Everlasting suppressed a snarl, and motioned to Blaze. *Begin, if you're ready.*

Blaze took a deep breath and knelt beside Sheppard, laying his feeding hand lightly on Moonwhite's belly, well below where the iratus queen gripped her. And that was another danger, Everlasing thought, feeding from an imperfect spot, but there were no better alternatives.

"Hang on," Sheppard said. He was pale and sweating lightly, but he edged his pistol forward until the muzzle very nearly touched the iratus queen's pulsing underbelly. "Ok. Ready when you are."

"I am ready," Blaze said. He closed his eyes for an instant, and set his claws. Moonwhite's body twitched, her head lolling to one side, but she made no sound. Blaze drank deeply, drawing the life-force from her so that her skin went pale and the bones showed stark under her skin. Everlasting flinched, unable not to see his own queen in that ravaged face, and still Blaze drank, while her hair faded from black to gray to white and her skin wrinkled like crumpled paper. Salt leaned forward, easing his illusion while emphasizing the withering husk, and Everlasting caught his breath. Had the iratus queen moved? Surely it would release her soon, any minute now.

Moonwhite looked dead, eaten, withered to nothing as one never saw a queen, and still Blaze drank, though his teeth were bared in fear and sorrow.

And then at last the iratus queen moved, withdrawing its claws with an angry rattle of carapace plates. Sheppard shoved his pistol forward and fired, and the iratus queen flipped off and away from Moonwhite. Forge struck out at it, knocking it further away, and the Marine Casey fired a long burst into it at point-blank range. The iratus queen disintegrated into a mess of chitin and ichored flesh, and Blaze flung himself forward, feeding the life back to his queen. Everlasting gave a gasp of relief, seeing her features plump and swell, and Sheppard pushed himself to his feet.

"That was well done," the Young Queen said, and he managed a wry smile.

"Let's hope it was worth it."

Blaze sat back on his heels, tears tracking his face beside the sensor pits. Before him, Moonwhite lay restored, even the gashes where the iratus queen had gripped her healed to faint and fading marks. But her eyes were still closed, though she seemed to be breathing normally enough.

Forge, Everlasting said.

The cleverman stooped beside her, first his off hand and then his feeding hand fluttering over her vital points. *She is alive and as far as I can tell unharmed,* he said at last.

So why doesn't she wake? Blaze demanded.

I don't know, Forge answered. "But I think we should move on — find shelter if we can, and then see

what we can do for her. And for him." He nodded to the
semi-conscious blade.

"Your queen," the Young Queen said. "She is not
recovered?"

"She needs more rest," Everlasting answered, and
hoped it was true. "In the meantime, we would be wise
to get away from here."

"And that," McKay said, "is the most sensible thing
anyone has said all day."

They made their way back down the mountain
toward the wrecked scout, Blaze carrying Moonwhite,
Everlasting and Forge taking turns to carry the blade.
He was starting to show signs of consciousness, soft pro-
tests when he was carried awkwardly and fluttering eyelids that gave Forge hope that he would come to himself
soon enough. They made camp on the ledge above the
wreck, upwind of any smells, and Salt and Everlasting
climbed down and came back with emergency shelters
undamaged by the crash. It was the work of an hour to
cut poles to stretch the swaths of fabric into a low tent
where Moonwhite could rest on a bed of soft branches,
and Forge sat with her while the others built a fire. He
could feel her pulse steady and slow under his thumb,
could feel the life circulating in her veins, but her eyes
were still closed, and even when he pressed cautiously
at her mind, she showed no signs of waking. The rav-
ages of the fever combined with the stress of its cure was
surely to blame, he thought. There was a good reason
that the iratus bugs were a last resort.

"Your queen."

He looked up to see the Lanteans' Young Queen standing outside the shelter's opening, politely out of reach.

"How is she?"

Forge hesitated, but there was little point in lying when the Young Queen could see for herself that Moonwhite was still unconscious. "She has not awakened, and I do not wish to push any harder, for fear I'll do more harm than good. We need to get her back to the hive as soon as possible."

"There will be a delay in that," the Young Queen said. "Our jumper is in use, ferrying patients from that village to Dr. Beckett's infirmary. They will not be able to come for us until morning, and possibly not then."

Forge suppressed a hiss, and Blaze loomed behind the Young Queen, scowling.

"We cannot wait that long."

To her credit, the Young Queen did not move away, just turned her head to look at him. "Can you say she is dying? The villagers are, and have no chance at all without our help."

"Let us call for our cruiser," Blaze answered promptly.

"Absolutely not," Sheppard interjected. "We had an agreement. No Wraith ships landing here."

"That was before we knew what had happened," Blaze said.

"We do not wish to imperil our treaty," the Young Queen said. "And I do not believe your queen is dying. Unlike the people of the village."

We can wait, Forge said, before Blaze could say more. He rested his feeding hand on Moonwhite's chest again, testing the life force. "She lives and is grown stronger. I don't think that we need worry that she hasn't woken. Yet."

Blaze snarled. *She is not your queen.*

She is my queen's sister, Forge snapped, *and my queen bade me serve her, and save her if I could. Do you doubt me?*

For a moment, he thought he had gone too far, and then Blaze shook his head. "No," he said aloud. "I will sit with her now. See if you can rouse the blade."

"Very well." Forge pushed himself to his feet. *Who is he, do you know?*

Bell, I think, or Adamant. Blaze settled himself at Moonwhite's side. *They were both with her.*

It was hard to tell one blade from another without the touch of their minds, particularly in hives like theirs that hewed closely to the physical canon of Night. Forge slipped past the Young Queen — she did not flinch from him, either — and went to where Everlasting and Salt were tending the strange blade. They had dragged him into a sitting position against a downed tree trunk, and his eyes were open, but still unfocused. On the far side of the fire, the Lanteans watched warily, and the Young Queen joined them, saying something too soft for him to hear. Forge put that out of his mind and crouched beside the stranger.

He looks better.

He has come round a little, Everlasting said, *but he needs to feed.*

Forge looked at the shredded coat and shirt, imagining what the wounds must have looked liked before he healed. The blade was clearly stronger than average to have survived at all.

He'll have to wait for that, Salt said, with a flash of wry humor, and Forge smiled in answer.

I can help him some. And perhaps that will bring him to full consciousness. Of course, he himself would need to feed soon then, there was only so much vitality he could spare, but he, at least, was in control of himself, and they would be returning to the hive soon enough. He went to his knees beside the strange blade and slid his feeding hand through the rips in coat and shirt, letting his handmouth just touch the blade's skin. The blade twitched at that, and tried to pull free, his eyelids fluttering open, and Forge let his hand relax.

Easy, he said. *Be easy. You're safe now.*

My queen… The mental voice was flawed and cracking, but still chimed like a bell.

She is alive and will be well, Forge said.

I do not know you.

I am of Light Breaking's hive, her Master of Sciences Biological.

She! Bell twitched again, trying to heave himself up and away from Forge's touch. *It was she who —* His eyes closed again, and he fell back, panting.

Forge swallowed a hiss. *I am here to help you. Let me feed you.*

I do not want the Gift from such as you, Bell snarled.

Salt laid his off hand on Forge's arm, urging silence. To Bell, he said, *Do you know me?*

There was a pause, Bell struggling to focus, and then he nodded. *Yes.*

*I belong to both hives, and neither — no storymaker

ever belongs to any one hive,* Salt said. *You know this.*

Bell nodded again. *Yes.*

I was sent to bear witness, Salt said. *Just as they were sent to rescue Moonwhite. You may trust them to help you this far.*

There was a long pause, Bell's eyelids flickering again, and then he nodded. *I consent.*

Forge flexed his feeding hand, setting his claws, and felt Bell's life-force flowing toward him, hot and sharp, tasting of fear and grief and thinned by exhaustion. He shifted his own focus, and fed it back to Bell, first the little that he had taken and then his own, pouring it out like salve on a burn. He saw Bell's features change, color coming back into his skin, and felt the moment his focus sharpened. Forge released him then, the first pangs of hunger tugging at his own chest, and sat back on his heels. *So.*

Bell pulled himself upright, settling himself more comfortably against the log, his movements for the first time entirely purposeful. *Thank you.*

It would be well, Everlasting said, looming over them so that Forge had to crane his neck to see the consort's face, *to tell us what happened.*

CHAPTER FOUR

SO FAR as he is able, Forge said, and laid a cautious hand on Bell's wrist.

The blade snatched it away. *Is there no one here who serves my queen?*

Her consort is here, Everlasting said.

I do not see him.

I am here. Blaze rose from his place at Moonwhite's side, though he kept himself between her and the others. *You may speak freely.*

"Hey." That was Sheppard, standing on the far side of the fire. "You want to let us in on this?"

Not particularly, Salt said, as though the thought escaped unbidden. Everlasting smiled in spite of himself, and Forge ducked his head to hide his amusement.

Humans, Bell said. *Lanteans? What are they doing here?*

They are here because you landed on a world given to them under Alabaster's treaty, Blaze answered. *And, yes, we will speak so that they can understand.*

Bell's mouth closed in a thin line. *I will not betray our queen's business to the Lanteans.*

You will do as I tell you, Blaze snapped. *And the first thing I want to know is how you came here.*

Forge looked across the fire to see Ronon looming behind Sheppard, and the cleverman McKay watchful to one side. The Young Queen pushed another branch into the fire, and looked up to meet his gaze, her eyes dark in the flickering light. *Speak aloud,* he said.

The cleverman is right, Blaze said, and switched to speech. "I ask you again, what happened? How did you come here?"

Bell bared teeth at him, though his weakness was still plain to see. A part of Forge's mind admired his courage even as he glanced sideways to see how the Lanteans were taking this.

"We came to visit their hive," Bell said sullenly, and jerked his head at Everlasting. "For what purpose, I do not know. The queen did not share that with me."

"Though you have been considerably in her company of late," Blaze said.

That had the familiar sound of rivalry, a consort working to keep down a rising favorite within the zenana, and Forge caught Everlasting's eye.

"Be that as it may," Everlasting said, and Blaze checked himself with visible impatience.

"So she did not share her mission. Very well. What do you know?"

"We came, we docked." Bell shrugged. "We waited while she went aboard alone. She returned, and we cast off again, to return to the hive."

"And then?" Blaze demanded.

Forge could see the Lanteans moving closer, spreading out so that they could see everyone's expressions more clearly. *Careful,* he said, and Salt touched his wrist.

Let them hear. It concerns them, too.

It would if they were Wraith. Forge paused, startled by the thought. If they were Wraith — if they were a species to be dealt with as though they were people — then this treaty was valid and the Lanteans had every right to be part of the discussion. And that was a weird and disturbing thought, and one he would not pursue just now.

Bell glanced unhappily at the Lanteans. "Once we left the hive, the queen complained that she was ill. We loaned her our strength, each of us in turn, but she did not heal, and then we all began to sicken. At that point, this was the nearest planet with a human population. We intended to land closer to the Stargate, but the ship itself seemed affected, and we crashed where you saw."

"And then?" Blaze prompted, when he seemed unwilling to continue.

We culled the village, Bell answered, with another look to the Lanteans. *Are you sure I should say that aloud?*

He should speak, Everlasting said, before Blaze could answer, and Blaze gave him a wary look. *We cannot hide it if it is true.*

They had seen no bodies in the village, and the villagers had not spoken of seeing Wraith. Forge hissed softly, and saw the same surprise in Salt's eyes.

"Speak," Blaze said.

On your head be it. Bell lifted his hands. "We, Silken and I, went to the village to cull. We fed ourselves and brought back humans for the queen to feed upon, but it only helped a little. Adamant had scouted while we were away, and said there was an iratus nest in the hills above us. The queen said that she would go there. And so we did."

It was, Forge thought, an entirely unsatisfactory narrative. *And the other blades? What happened to them?*

An excellent question, Everlasting said.

"Well?" Blaze glared at Bell. "How did the others die?"

"They gave their lives for the queen, so that she would be strong enough to endure the iratus bite," Bell said.

"And yet you live," Salt said.

"She tried to leave us enough alive that she could restore us when she was healed," Bell answered. "That is our queen's way, not to waste any blade's life."

And our queen does not endanger her people in the first place, Forge thought, but that was not something he could say aloud without starting the fight that Bell was begging for. He chose his words carefully. "This is not entirely clear to me. The Lanteans said the village was not culled."

"And why would they tell us the truth?" Bell snarled.

"Why would they not?" Everlasting answered. "Such a lie would hardly be to their advantage."

"Unless they would prefer to make alliance with your queen," Bell said, "a thing which my queen would never have tolerated."

"To the best of my knowledge," Everlasting said, his eyes on Blaze, "our queen had not yet made up her mind about Alabaster's offer. We had no dealings with the Lanteans until this moment."

"Nor had our queen made a decision," Blaze said, but his tone was less certain than his words. "And yet…"

"She was well when she left our hive," Bell said. "And she was well when we arrived on yours. It was only after we left that she grew ill."

"If that is an accusation," Everlasting said, his voice cold, "speak plainly."

"Isn't that plain enough?" Bell stretched out his hand to Blaze. "I say our queen was infected aboard their hive, and if they have no sickness, then how can it be anything but a direct attack?"

"Hang on," Sheppard said, from the far side of the fire, and Forge saw the Young Queen rise to her feet frowning.

Everlasting ignored him, his attention on Blaze. "You spoke with my queen yourself. You know she is worried for her sister."

"So I did." Blaze's expression was unreadable. "And yet. Bell raises some interesting points."

"Let us ask the Lanteans," Forge said. Both consorts turned on him, snarling, and he made himself face them without flinching. "If there were no bodies found, either here or in the woods — then perhaps the fever has confused Bell's mind."

"We didn't search the woods," Blaze said, but Forge thought he relaxed just a little.

"Sheppard," Everlasting said. "You've heard what this one says. Could there have been Wraith in the village — could one of us have culled without your knowing it?"

Sheppard looked at the Young Queen, who gave a fractional shrug. "I don't know. It depends on how sick people were, where your man took his prisoners, whether there was anyone left alive who knew about it."

"The death toll was high," McKay said. "And at least half the people in that hall were unconscious. It's just possible that everyone who had contact with the Wraith, or knew about it, wasn't able to talk."

"I don't believe it," Ronon said flatly. "Word would

spread. And that kid wasn't scared. Not the way he would have been if there'd been a culling."

"I agree with Ronon," the Young Queen said. "Perhaps your man culled on the outskirts, though? There were some isolated houses."

"Well?" Blaze looked at Bell, who shrugged.

"We did not enter the village, no. There was no need."

"This makes — not enough sense," Everlasting said.

"It makes entirely good sense," Bell said. "Your queen tried to kill ours."

"She did not." Everlasting spread his hands, showing off-hand and feeding hand together, his eyes on Blaze. "You spoke to our queen —"

"More to the point," Salt said, "would she have sent her Consort and her Master of Sciences Biological, knowing that if anyone had survived the crash her plan would come to light?"

Blaze drew a long breath. "Sheppard. Can your people inquire of the villagers, find out if there was a culling here?"

"We can ask," Sheppard said. "McKay. See what Beckett can do."

"On it," McKay answered, and withdrew, muttering into his communications gear.

"What more proof do you want?" Everlasting asked. Blaze snarled but did not answer.

"You are both forgetting something," Salt said. "When the queen awakens, she can tell you herself what happened."

Both consorts relaxed slightly, but Bell shook his head. "We should not wait. We should take her to *Nimble* now, return her to the hive where she can be cared for properly."

"*Nimble* will never fly again," Blaze said. "My own brother lies dead at the controls. We must depend on the Lanteans to return us to the Stargate."

"Which we'll do as soon as we can," Sheppard said, with another of his uneasy smiles. "Just not tonight."

"So you have said." Blaze took a deep breath. "I will stay with my queen tonight, and you, Bell, will keep watch with me. In the morning we will consider further."

Everlasting dipped his head. "A wise plan. Forge and I will be here, where you can see us."

"And I," Salt said, with some exasperation, "will tend the fire. Here. Where everyone can see."

"And we'll just watch all of you from over here," Sheppard said. "Should be a fun night."

The night passed more swiftly than Blaze had believed possible. Moonwhite still slept, cushioned on her nest of branches; when he touched her hand, her skin was cool and faintly damp, and the life-force moved steadily within her. And yet she did not wake. Bell lay just outside the shelter's entrance, so that anyone who tried to enter would have to step over him, drowsing in the semi-trance that passed for a blade's sleep in time of danger. Blaze didn't know what to make of his story. On the one hand, it was what he himself had feared from the beginning, that Light Breaking had decided to kill her sister rather than continue to argue about their best course. History was full of such stories, sisters who slew each other for control of their hives, daughters who killed mothers, mothers who killed daughters, and always for what seemed at the time to be good reasons. Moonwhite herself was capable of making such a choice, if pushed to it, and he did not love her less because of that.

And yet. Everlasting believed he was telling the truth, and Blaze did not believe that Light Breaking would lie to him so directly. If Moonwhite had done the same to him, told him a lie and sent him to another hive to uphold it — it was a betrayal, and he did not think either sister would choose that course. He and Everlasting had been friends, before they chose different queens, he had even rescued Everlasting once, when a culling had gone badly wrong, and both Moonwhite and Light Breaking had found that relationship useful. As Light Breaking found it now.

It was possible that Bell's memories were confused. That could happen when a person was wounded and starved, actual events tangling, remembered out of order or only in part. It was even possible to mistake intent for action, to have planned a thing and been sure one accomplished it, only to discover that it was all illusion. And certainly Bell had been terribly injured — and by what? Blaze frowned, considering the pattern of slashes across the front of Bell's coat. There was more damage than he would have expected from the attack of even a swarm of iratus — they went for the exposed flesh of neck and face for preference, not the usually-covered center of the body — and the pattern didn't really fit injuries suffered in the crash itself. Perhaps the humans they had taken had fought back? That seemed to be the best explanation.

He rested his hand on Moonwhite's chest, the exposed skin pale as marble in the firelight. The marks where the iratus queen had gripped her were long healed, not even a shadow to mar that perfection. He could feel her life-force flowing strongly — his own strength, at least in part, and gladly given. Light Breaking was the more out-going of the sisters, but Moonwhite's quieter strength had drawn him like a moon draws the tide. He stroked her cheek, daring a caress she would barely have tolerated even in the privacy of her own bedchamber.

Come back, beloved, he whispered, barely the thread of a thought to lie against her mind. For a moment, he thought she stirred, eyelids flickering, but her thoughts dropped away from him, sinking into darkness deeper than sleep. He blinked hard, his eyes stinging with tears he would not shed, and arranged her more comfortably on her bed of branches.

The Lanteans were active with the sunrise, building up the fire that Salt had allowed to burn down and fetching water to begin their own meals. Forge brought water without being asked, and Blaze took his share with only a momentary pang of distrust. If Everlasting wanted to be rid of him, he would not make that move under the Lanteans' eye. Moonwhite slept still, though he thought when he reached out to her that she was closer to consciousness than she had been.

What next? he asked Everlasting, as they stretched in the rising warmth.

Return to your hive as quickly as we may? Everlasting shrugged. *That would be my choice.*

*The Lanteans said they would bring their jumper back

as soon as they could,* Blaze said, *but I don't see it.*

"Hey." That was Sheppard, straightening from his meal. "I've got some good news and some bad news. Which do you want first?"

Blaze looked at Everlasting, who shrugged. "Begin with the bad, and perhaps it will indeed get better."

"You know, I would have bet on your being a good-news-first kind of guy," Sheppard said. "Anyway. Bad news it is. We won't have the use of a jumper until this afternoon, and maybe not then."

Blaze snarled. "You made us a promise, Sheppard."

"They're carrying the sickest people in for treatment at Beckett's clinic," Sheppard answered. "And then they'll need to be decontaminated before we ride in them. That takes time. You want to hear the good news?"

Blaze's feeding hand twitched, but he made himself nod. "Go on."

"Beckett's people managed to ask some questions overnight. Turns out that a couple of people remember a man from the village coming back with a story of a wrecked Wraith ship, and there was talk about hiding out away from the village in case there was a culling — and some discussion of whether or not they should try to salvage anything." Sheppard smiled tightly. "But nobody says they know anything about anybody being eaten."

Blaze cocked his head, considering. "Is everyone accounted for? In the village, I mean."

"No." Sheppard's smile eased, as though that was the question he'd hoped for.

"So it proves nothing either way," Everlasting said.

"It's suggestive," Blaze said. Out of the corner of his

eye, he could see Bell take up his guard outside the queen's shelter, and lifted a hand to beckon to him. "We have questions."

"I should remain here," Bell protested.

"You can leave her long enough to speak to me," Blaze said, controlling his annoyance with an effort. "No other will approach her."

Bell came reluctantly to join them, positioning himself so that he could see anyone approaching the queen's shelter. "What is it?"

"You said you culled the nearby village," Blaze said. "Or was it houses nearby?"

Bell hesitated, for the first time since they had found him looking less certain of himself. "It wasn't the village, but outlying — a farmstead, maybe? There were four kine in the house, there was no need to seek further."

"And you are certain you culled?" Blaze did his best to ignore the look on Sheppard's face. "You didn't plan it, and then choose to seek the iratus nest instead?"

Bell hesitated again. "I — believe so? I was ill."

"And injured," Everlasting said. "How did that happen?"

Bell looked down at his coat as though seeing the rips and tears for the first time. "I don't know. I don't remember."

"In which case, he may very well not remember whether he culled or not," Blaze said.

"Does that happen often?" Sheppard asked. "Just forgetting that you ate someone? Because that could be kind of awkward."

"When someone is badly injured, memories blur," Everlasting said impatiently. "Things are remembered incorrectly. Does that never happen with humans?"

Sheppard's face changed. "Yeah. Sometimes."

"If we are stranded here another day," Blaze said slowly, "I would like to see if we could find that farmstead, or the bodies that were fed upon. I do not distrust you," he added, before Bell could protest, "but I would like more clarity in this picture."

Bell subsided, controlling his thoughts well enough that Blaze did not have to notice his disagreement.

"What exactly do you have in mind?" Sheppard asked.

"The Consort and I should search," Blaze said, nodding at Everlasting. "As I have said. You would, of course, be welcome to accompany us."

Everlasting smiled at that, and Sheppard looked distinctly sour. "Yeah, I just bet." He chewed his lower lip for a moment. "Teyla! Come here a minute, will you?"

The Young Queen set aside her rations and came to join them. Of all the humans, she looked least troubled by her night under the stars, sleek and calm as ever.

"These guys want to go looking for the bodies of the people that got fed on," Sheppard said. "I was thinking I'd take McKay, unless you wanted to come."

The Young Queen considered the question. "I think that is a good plan. There is much here that does not make sense. Yes, take Rodney. I will stay here with Ronon and — Casey?"

Sheppard nodded. "Yeah. And Hernandez. Just in case the queen wakes up hungry."

"A reasonable precaution," the Young Queen said.

In the end, it was agreed that Bell would guard the queen while Forge kept an eye on her condition, and

Everlasting and Blaze would try to make sense of a story Bell admitted was no longer entirely clear. There was no avoiding Sheppard's company, or that of the cleverman McKay, but when Blaze complained privately, Everlasting merely shrugged.

Perhaps it is as well to have witnesses. No one can say they are partial.

That was true, though it was a sobering thought. But there was no point in protesting, and Blaze led them back up the slope to the first mark they'd found. He paused there, trying to make sense of the images Bell had shared, and Sheppard rested his hands on the butt of his weapon.

"You know, I'm still not getting this. Your queen left a trail up to the iratus bugs, right? Coming from the ship? So if your guys did feed, why didn't we find the bodies there?"

"That's assuming they were camped at the ship," McKay said. "Were they?"

Everlasting shrugged, and Blaze said, "We think so. Or, rather, her blade says so."

"It would make sense," Everlasting said. "It is shelter, and I would expect to have been found sooner rather than later."

"But they were all sick," McKay said. "Right? And I'm guessing all the communications equipment was smashed in the crash."

"Correct," Everlasting said.

Blaze made an effort not to bare his teeth. The curiosity of clevermen was their most useful trait, but there were times, he felt, when it should be restrained.

"So why wouldn't they at least have moved the body?" McKay looked as though that personally offended him. "I can't see camping out in a decaying wreck with a dead man just hanging over the controls."

He has a point, Everlasting said.

Bell said nothing of a camp, Blaze answered.

Yes, but there seems to be a great deal he doesn't remember, Everlasting said.

"If you've got something to say," Sheppard said, "let's share it with the class."

Blaze blinked, but decided he didn't need to understand the idiom to know what the Lantean meant. "He said we should follow the ridge to find the farmstead. If there was a camp, perhaps it will be on that line as well."

They tracked west along the top of the ridge, following what Blaze could understand of Bell's memories. The blade had clearly been unwell, the images wavering and highly colored, tasting of iron and ash. But, yes, there was the twisted tree, split by lightning, only one branch still bearing a defiant cluster of dark leaves.

"There," he said, pointing. "If we bear south, down the ridge, we should find a dry stream, and then the farmstead."

There were more signs of a human presence as they walked, trails worn in the scrub that led to what Blaze guessed would be good hunting spots, and as they crossed the stream, dry except for a trickle of water at its very center, they began to see scars where something had grazed on the vegetation. Even as he thought that, there was a rustle in the undergrowth, and a shaggy four-legged creature bolted from shelter and charged up the hill, three smaller versions of itself scampering in its wake.

McKay turned, looking as startled as the rest of them. "That looked — was that a goat?"

"Anything's possible," Sheppard answered. "Looks like we're getting closer."

Blaze pressed on, following a trail that widened until it was easily big enough for two to walk abreast. The trees were taller here, and straighter, not shaped by the winter winds, and he was unsurprised to see the path open out into a small clearing. A house stood there, low and turf-roofed, and another of the shaggy animals was standing on the rooftree, grazing on the flower-studded grass. They had come from the fenced enclosure, Blaze guessed, but the gate stood open, the three-sided shed empty except for a long trough. There was no smoke from the chimney, and the field behind the house looked as though it had not been tended in some days.

Sheppard held up his hand. "Hello! Anybody home?"

The shout startled a flock of blue-winged birds that rose out of the field in a chattering crowd, but there was no other answer.

There is no one here, Everlasting said.

Not alive, Blaze answered. He said aloud, "If there were humans here, they would not let the birds take their crop."

"I hate to say it, but I think you're right." Sheppard moved out into the clearing. "Hello? Anyone?"

There was no answer, not even birds this time, and Sheppard and McKay exchanged unhappy looks.

"Better check it out," Sheppard said, and McKay shook his head.

"You know, investigating alien plagues is really outside my field of expertise."

"Beckett's shot should be good enough," Sheppard answered, and headed for the door.

"Should be isn't the same as definitely," McKay said, but copied him.

Blaze followed them both, Everlasting at his heels, and tipped his face to the breeze to try to get a sense of what might be waiting for them. There was no taint of death, only the sour scent of human habitation, unwashed bodies and animals, and he couldn't help glancing back at Everlasting. *I don't believe that they were here.*

Nor I. Though it's possible Bell or one of the others found the place and planned to cull, but were too weak to manage.

"Hello," Sheppard called again, and stuck his head through the narrow door. "Hello?" He pulled back a moment later. "There's nobody there, and it looks to me like they packed up and left."

"Let me see," Blaze said, and the Lanteans moved out of his way.

The interior of the house was dark and smelled even more strongly of animals and humans, but the central hearth was empty, the ashes spread to be sure no sparks were left, and there were no pots on the shelves. The bedstead had been stripped of blankets, though the mattress remained, and there was a single wooden chest against the side wall. Blaze opened it, and found it empty except for a few bits of wood. The larder was empty, even the earthenware crock as large as a child scraped clean of all but a handful of grain. Abandoned, yes, but the owners had had time to pack their things.

Gone, he said, to Everlasting, sharing the image, and felt the other consort's agreement. He stepped back out into the sunlight and the clean air, and said aloud, "They have left and taken their goods, I agree. Possibly for fear of us —"

"You can't blame them for that," Sheppard said.

"But there was no culling here."

"I agree," Everlasting said. "So — your man dreamed it in his fever?"

Blaze shook his head. "I don't know. It doesn't make sense."

"My guess is they were either running from you," Sheppard said, "or someone came down with the fever and they were trying to take them to the village."

That was certainly possible. Blaze cast around, circling the house and the open pen, but the ground was hard and dry, showing no footsteps.

"If they saw the scout crash," McKay said, "they might have known what it was, or they just might not have wanted to take chances, given that any ship that crash-lands on any planet around here is likely to be unfriendly. So they packed up —"

"And turned their livestock loose," Sheppard said.

"Yes, and let the goats out, probably because trying to herd goats through a forest is a lot harder than carrying bundles of food, and high-tailed it for the village." McKay let out his breath. "Though that's still a hard walk. And that might rule out fever —"

"No," Everlasting said. "Look here. They had a cart."

Blaze came to join him, stared at the familiar double track where wheels had crossed another nearly-dry stream. "Which might mean they were indeed ill? Or simply afraid."

"I don't know that it matters much," Sheppard said. "But it does mean your guys didn't feed here."

And if they didn't feed here, they didn't feed at all. And that meant — what? That Bell was mistaken? Certainly he had taken injuries serious enough to affect his memory. Or was Everlasting lying, playing some long and complicated game to put his queen in control of her sister's hive? Neither alternative made sense, and he turned to look back up the ridge, trying to see where they were in relation to the iratus hive. "I would very much like to know how the other blades died."

"They were fed upon, surely," Everlasting answered.

"But when, and by whom?" Blaze shaded his eyes as though that would help him see further between the trees.

"Your queen?" Everlasting's voice was less certain than his words.

"So I thought."

"So Bell said."

"If his memory can be trusted," Blaze said. "And it seems we have proof that it cannot."

"Wait a minute," McKay said. "Are you — you're not seriously considering going back to that nest, are you?"

"I admit that it would be dangerous," Blaze began, and Everlasting shook his head.

"Dangerous and foolish — foolhardy. With their queen dead, they will be on a hair trigger, ready to swarm anything that crosses their webs. And anyway, what could you hope to see? They were drained of life, that was clear."

Everlasting was right, Blaze thought. There was no way to tell who had devoured those blades, merely that they had been fed upon, and certainly the most logical person to have done so was Moonwhite. She had every right to demand that last service, and certainly any blade of hers would have been glad to give her his life.

"I can't believe I'm saying this," Sheppard said, "but I'm with him." He jerked his thumb at Everlasting. "I think it's a really bad idea to go back to that nest."

"I suppose you're right," Blaze said. "Let us return." As they made their way back to the camp, though, a new thought nagged at him: what — or who — had attacked Bell?

They made their way back to the camp, detouring through the woods to search for any further signs of Moonwhite's party. Everlasting was not surprised to find none, except of course for the markers they had left to point the way toward the iratus nest. If Bell's condition was any indication, the entire group had been deathly ill — and how exactly had they been exposed to the blood fever? If they had fed on any humans, it would have been easy to trace the contagion there, and argue that the Lanteans had it backwards, that the fever had been indigenous to Tesierit and the Wraith had contracted it from them. But Bell swore Moonwhite had been sick before *Nimble* crashed — and indeed, it was hard to account for the crash in any way other than that the crew or the ship itself was ill. Unless there had been sabotage? Not on Light Breaking's hive, he didn't believe that Light Breaking would have sent him here if she had meant to kill her sister, but on Moonwhite's hive? Among some other, disaffected faction? One of Alabaster's people? That made the most sense, except that he could see no way for any of Alabaster's people to gain access to Moonwhite's hive. Perhaps there had been a visit he didn't know about? He would have to ask Blaze once they returned.

Nothing had changed when they returned to the camp, except that the fire had been allowed to die down to coals, and the Lanteans had constructed a set of comfortable-looking three-sided shelters. Bell still squatted in the doorway of Moonwhite's shelter, and Blaze lifted his head uneasily.

Any change?

She still sleeps, Bell answered, and Forge rose from where he had been sitting by the fire.

I might be able to do something for her, but your man will not let me see.

Not without the Consort's order, Bell said, and his tone added, *and not even then.*

It might not be a bad idea, Everlasting said, after a moment, and Bell snarled at him.

And see you harm her further? Over my dead body.

That could be arranged, Forge snapped, and shook himself hard. *No. Our queen would not wish it. Though he has been very difficult all day.*

I do not trust them, Bell said stubbornly.

Blaze walked to the door of the shelter and stood for a moment, staring down at the queen's motionless body. Everlasting couldn't see his expression, but he could feel the sudden sorrow, quickly suppressed. *Is she —?* he began, and Blaze shook himself.

Unchanged. Which worries me. She should have begun to heal by now.

So she should, Everlasting thought. He said, carefully, *Forge is a skilled healer. Perhaps he —*

Blaze shook his head. *I think we will wait a little longer before we try that.*

As you wish. Everlasting seated himself on the length of log, and Forge brought him fresh water. The air here was relatively dry, and Everlasting was glad to drink and splash the moisture on his face.

Did you really think the consort would trust you? Bell hissed.

Be silent, Blaze said.

I will not. Bell rose to his feet, though he did not move from the opening of the shelter. *Consort, they are responsible for our queen's state. You must do something.*

Such as? Blaze cocked his head to one side, but kept his eyes on Everlasting.

Make them tell what they have done, Bell said. *That is their cleverman, he must know.*

I have done nothing, Forge snapped, and Everlasting rose to his feet, meeting Blaze stare for stare.

Do you call me a liar, Consort?

There was a clatter of weapons from the other side of the fire, and Sheppard said, "Hang on. What's the problem here?"

Blaze ignored them, but Bell burst out, "They are the ones who have harmed our queen. It's their fault."

"I'm not entirely sure that's the case," McKay said. "I

mean, how do you figure that? They weren't even there when your queen got sick, right?"

Blaze's eyes flickered. "So they say."

"It is true," Everlasting said.

"And I," Forge said, "was on Alabaster's hive. I had just returned when you spoke to our queen — as you well know."

"That's what she told me," Blaze said, his voice remote.

"And you doubt her word?" Everlasting flexed his feeding hand in spite of himself, and Blaze showed teeth in answer.

"Wait a minute," Sheppard said. "Wait just a minute here. Let's nobody make any unfortunate choices."

"This is not your concern," Blaze said.

"Yeah, actually, it is," Sheppard said. "You're here under our protection, like it or not, and we intend to send you back to your hives unharmed, because we don't want to be blamed for anything that happens to you. Any of you."

"I am sure Alabaster would absolve you," Blaze said.

"I don't really care what Alabaster thinks," Sheppard said.

The Young Queen said, "I am still entirely unsure what happened to your queen."

Blaze blinked, and when he answered, his tone was more conciliatory. "Nor am I."

"She was poisoned on their hive," Bell said, stubbornly. "She must have been; she fell ill as soon as she came back aboard. We thought we could make it back to our hive, but she was too ill — we were all too ill. When we crashed —" He stopped, shaking his head. "I am sure we culled so that she could feed. But you tell me we did not?"

"There were no bodies," Blaze said. "The villagers left of their own will."

"Then — I don't know. I was ill, too, fevered." Bell shook his head. "But we carried our queen into the hills so that she could heal. And she was healed. Or she will be."

"What happened to the other blades?" Salt asked. It was the first time he'd spoken in this argument, and Everlasting twitched in spite of himself.

"What concern is it of yours?" Bell said.

"He is as much of our hive as theirs," Blaze said. "Answer the question."

Bell dipped his head. "I don't know. I don't remember. I — our queen planned to feed on them, on all of us, so that she could survive the iratus queen's cure, and then she would restore us."

It was possible, Everlasting thought. Everything in Bell's story was possible, and yet none of it could be proved.

"I will point out," Salt said mildly, "that this is Light Breaking's consort and her chief cleverman. She would not risk them lightly."

"To kill a queen is not a light thing," Blaze answered.

Everlasting took a step forward. "My queen sent me in good faith." He conjured up the memory of a crashed Dart and a mob of humans armed with Genii weapons, the pain of a dozen wounds and the certainty that he had made one mistake too many. Blaze had come for him then, a flight of Darts swooping past to drive back the human mob, and then a culling beam to rescue him and the only other survivor. That had been in Edge's day, and Blaze had even spoken up for him before the queen. He laid that memory like an offering between them, his failure as much of an exposure as a bared chest. *I am in your debt, and you know it. I give you my word, on my own honor, and the debt between us, my queen has no wish to see your queen dead. And I will prove it to you, if you wish, by heart-and-hand.*

He heard Forge hiss at that, but did not look back. Heart-and-hand was an old ritual, left over from the wars with the Ancients, when there had been enough different battles on different fronts that blades negotiated for their queens. Two blades laid their feeding hands against each other's hearts and set claws, skin to skin and life forces mingling, a terrible and dangerous intimacy of blood and mind. It did not preclude lying — a strong-minded blade could make a weaker see what he wished — but it was punishingly hard. And Blaze knew him well enough that Everlasting wasn't sure he could have fooled him if he had wanted to.

Blaze slowly shook his head. *No. I will not risk your life, not when we may need all of us to protect our queen from the Lanteans. But — I am honored by the offer.*

What now? Bell asked, and sounded genuinely bewildered. *What do we do, Consort?*

"We will keep the queen safe, you and I," Blaze said aloud, "and wait for her to wake. Her story will clarify — many things."

Everlasting dipped his head in acknowledgement. "And I and mine will — leave you to it. Until you need us."

"Very well," Blaze answered, and ducked into the shelter to settle himself beside his queen.

Forge eased closer to the fire, careful to position himself so that he could keep both Bell and Blaze in sight. The sun was setting, the shadows thick under the trees and the air already touched with night's chill. The Lanteans were gathered in a huddle on the far side of the fire: they had already announced that their jumper would not be arriving until morning — a palpable lie, Forge considered, but one they could not argue with. Which meant that they were trapped with a hostile consort and the Lanteans for another night, a circumstance he hoped they would not regret.

He poured himself a cup of water, and drank carefully. The air in the mountains was uncomfortably dry, leaving his lips cracked and the tender skin of his handmouth sore and raw. He cupped his hands around his mouth, breathing new moisture into them, then poured another cup of water and crossed to Moonwhite's shelter. Blaze blocked his way, his expression unreadable, and Forge held out the cup.

Your queen should drink.

If she can. Blaze took the cup and sniffed it, lips parted to help his sensor pits work.

I will taste it if you like, Forge said, wearily, and Blaze handed the cup to him.

Drink, then.

Will you let me see her? Forge took a long drink of the water, lifting his chin so that Blaze could see his throat working as he swallowed. *I may be able to help her.*

Blaze accepted the cup again. *Perhaps later.*

At least it was not complete refusal. Forge said carefully, *Is there any change?*

For a moment, he thought Blaze would ignore him, but then the consort sighed. *Not much. And what there is — it's so small I'm afraid it's wishful thinking.*

I could tell you that, Forge thought, but he understood well enough why Blaze might not want to know. *We will return to our ships tomorrow.*

Unless the Lanteans delay further. Blaze's mouth twitched in a wry, unwilling smile. *Bell thinks we should take them now and steal their ship. Or summon our own, and fight the Lanteans for it. And when I pointed out that folly, he said perhaps we should sneak away to signal them, though I'm not sure how he thinks we'd do that, given that Nimble's systems are dead and it's the Mothers only know how far back to the Stargate.*

The Lantean ships could only be crewed by descendants of the Ancestors who bore their particular genetic signature: every Wraith knew that, and nobody here wanted to fight the Lanteans and their rapid-fire weapons. As for stealth —Bell should know best of any of them how far they were from the Stargate. Did he expect them to walk back, carrying the queen? *He is… volatile,* Forge said, and surprised a flash of amusement from the consort.

Undeniable. Blaze sobered instantly. *We will wait,* he said, and ducked back into the shelter.

Forge sighed and turned back to the fire. He had done the best he could — he would ask again later, in the morning, perhaps, when the dark didn't loom ahead of them. Salt prodded the fire with a branch stripped from one of the smaller trees, turning it until the res-in-filled nubs that tipped each branch popped and burst into spark and sudden flame, gone as quickly as it flared.

No luck? he asked, not taking his eyes from the burning branch.

Not yet. Forge softened his thoughts, not wanting to share them with Bell, still crouching outside the shelter. *Though perhaps tomorrow, if she's no better.*

I am worried that she doesn't wake.

So am I. Forge swallowed his anger, knowing it was born of fear, said, more moderately, *I don't know what's wrong. She seems free of the fever — she shows no symp-toms, and none of us are sick, nor the Lanteans; it's a rough measure, but accurate enough. That argues that the iratus cure worked, but she should have awakened as soon as the iratus queen was removed.*

Suppose the cure wasn't complete when we killed the queen? Everlasting had come up on them so silently that Forge started, and Salt bared teeth in a reflexive hiss.

It's possible, Forge said. *In which case presumably she will wake when her own systems have finished heal-ing her, but — I would be happier if she was on her own hive, with her own clevermen to tend her.*

Is there anything else it could be? The last of the resinous nubs had burned out; Salt pulled the branch from the fire, stubbed out the last ember, and began idly tracing a six by six grid in the dirt.

Too many things, Forge said. *And, while I under-stand it — I can't help if I can't examine her.*

You examined her before, Everlasting said. *When

she was brought out of the cave. Surely that gives you some idea.*

Forge shook his head. *What I felt then was mostly the iratus taint.* He closed his eyes, remembering. *The touch of fever beneath that, but it was almost gone. She was almost entirely well then. And that only makes it more confusing.*

Figure out something, if you can. In the fire, a pile of branches collapsed into sparks and ash, and Everlasting kicked a stray chunk back into the safety of the ring.

I'll do what I can, Forge said.

Everlasting hunched one shoulder and moved away.

The situation is troubling, Salt offered, after a moment. He reached into his pocket and produced a handful of dice and counters. Forge considered him for a moment — was this really the time? — but seated himself cross-legged opposite the storymaker.

It is that.

Salt divided the counters into two sets of six, and handed one across. *If you'd like, I'll speak to Blaze, see if I can't persuade him to let you examine his queen.*

It couldn't hurt, Forge said, and set his opening counters in position, clustered in the corners on his side of the board. *There's another thing you could do, possibly.*

Oh? Salt massed his pieces in the center of his board, the standard countermove.

You're a storymaker, Forge said. *And a son of Osprey. You can touch our minds — can't you see the truth of what happened?* Salt was already shaking his head, and Forge stopped, his first move half finished.

You can't or you won't?

Can't, Salt said, and nodded to the improvised board. *Go on.*

Forge sighed, and moved the second marker. A conventional opening, but his mind wasn't really on the game. *I'm not sure I — understand.* He deliberately did not say 'believe,' but thought Salt understood his intent well enough.

Salt moved a piece in answer. *I am a storymaker,* he said, *and a son of Osprey — most storymakers have Osprey strongly in their line. My gift is to make you see, not to see what you would hide. It is all illusion, whether I tell a tale of ages past or wreathe iratus bugs in a dream of winter fog. It is the sons of Night who can bend minds to their will, though I will admit that skill has grown weaker over the years.*

Forge scowled. This was old history; he wasn't sure he shouldn't be offended to have it recited to him. And yet Salt was not one to indulge in gratuitous offense. He glanced at the board to hide his confusion, and blinked as he recognized the configuration. They had fallen — no, Salt had deliberately played the move that brought the pieces into the Doubled-Knife, where either of the usual responses would lead to a convoluted endgame that would leave Salt with no worse than a stalemate. And if that was a message... *The only blade of Night here is Bell.*

Salt dipped his head.

It took all Forge's willpower not to reach across the makeshift board and shake the answer out of the storymaker. *What is it you've found?*

Nothing. Which is why I have said nothing until now. Salt shrugged. *He feels honest enough, what I've touched of his mind. But he is a blade of Night, and his story makes no sense. Your move.*

Forge shifted counters without thinking. If Bell lied — if he had made the rest of his party believe in illness — no, it was unlikely any blade would be stronger than a queen of Night's line. Moonwhite would surely have realized what was happening if Bell had tried to influence her that way. Of course, his fellow blades were more susceptible, and all the more so if they were concentrating on their queen. And certainly Bell had done his best to convince the rest of them that he had culled, though he had not managed to convince anyone. *I didn't — I don't believe he's tried to shape our thoughts. That we would have noticed.*

Salt moved a counter, locking an entire quadrant of the board. *Yes. I think so. And yet.*

Forge stared at the pieces, doubly frustrated. Bell's story made no sense as it stood, and yet a version in which he coerced — not Moonwhite, he wouldn't be strong enough even if he dared, and there was no cause to oppose her, but perhaps his fellow blades — that made only a little more sense. And it all faltered on the lack of motive. *It makes no sense,* he said again, and Salt nodded.

No. But if this were my story, and I were locked — He gestured at the board with his off hand. *That is where I would look to solve it.*

This is no one's tale, Forge said, and hoped that was true.

CHAPTER FIVE

EVERLASTING deliberately turned his back on the other Wraith, walking as far away from them as he could without encroaching on the Lanteans' side of the fire. Nothing made sense, neither Bell's story nor his own queen's orders, or at least not unless one of them was lying. He didn't believe it was Light Breaking, and yet he could see no reason for Bell to lie. Out of the corner of his eye, he could see Forge and Salt moving counters in a quick game of blades, and it took all his willpower not to snarl at them to do something more useful. On the far side of the fire, Ronon and Hernandez were threading fist-sized vegetables on sticks and setting them to roast in the coals, sending up puffs of aromatic steam as the husks began to char.

Sheppard moved toward him, came to stand just out of reach. "Got a minute?"

Everlasting tipped his head to one side. "Yes?"

"I —" Sheppard glanced over his shoulder, including the Young Queen in his gaze. "We were wondering what you made of this."

"You've seen what I've seen," Everlasting answered.

"Yeah, but I don't know what you know. I'm asking what you think happened."

"I don't know."

"You've got to have some idea." Sheppard squinted at him as though the smoke from the fire hurt his eyes. The Young Queen took a step closer, though she was careful not to touch him.

"We are concerned that your queen has not yet awakened. Is it possible that there is more wrong than the effects of blood fever?"

Sheppard gave her a look as though he hadn't expected her to join the conversation, but said nothing.

Everlasting shrugged. "It's possible. My fellow consort is unwilling to let our cleverman examine her more closely."

"He does not trust you," the Young Queen said.

"I don't trust him," Everlasting answered. "Not entirely. Though I do not see what advantage this brings them."

"I had wondered that as well," the Young Queen said, with a smile that softened the strong lines of her face and did not reassure him at all.

"What I was wondering was what happened to the guy you rescued," Sheppard said. "How he got hurt in the first place — you can't miss that his coat's cut to ribbons."

"He says he doesn't remember," Everlasting said.

"Yeah," Sheppard said, with a lifted eyebrow, and Everlasting grinned in spite of himself.

"But I can't force him to tell the truth, he's not my man. And it's possible that he truly doesn't remember, or doesn't remember clearly —"

"He says his queen was sick, and they landed here to cull, right?" Sheppard said. "And then that all went wrong and she had to go to the iratus bugs to see if the queen would cure her."

"Yes." Everlasting nodded, but his eyes were on the Young Queen, still at Sheppard's side.

"That does not explain what happened to the other blades," she said. "Or to Bell himself. Or indeed how your queen was exposed to the fever."

"No, it doesn't. Though my queen was not behind it."
This time Everlasting couldn't quite conceal his anger,
but the Young Queen merely smiled.

"I propose a different interpretation," she said. "A sim-
pler one. Suppose Bell were the culprit."

"Impossible!" Everlasting drew himself up, shocked.
"He is a loyal blade —" He stopped then, unable to continue. He didn't know Bell, didn't know his history;
Blaze would know, but this was an awkward question
to ask of any consort, and he wasn't willing to lose all
good will over something so unlikely.

"Is it?" The Young Queen tipped her head in turn.
"Many impossible things have been done lately."

"It makes more sense that way," Sheppard said. "Your
guy infects the queen, and probably everyone else on
the ship, and that forces them to put down here. And I'd
bet he was the guy to suggest the iratus bugs, because
my understanding is, that doesn't work all the time."

"It does not." Everlasting listened in horrified fasci-
nation, unable to deny that the pieces fit.

"So he talks them into going up into the hills, the
queen and the rest of the blades, and then — there's a
fight. Maybe something he does tips them off, I don't
know, but that's how he gets hurt, and how those other
guys get fed on. Only he's hurt too bad himself, and
passes out by the cave entrance. And we found him
before he could finish the job."

"It's not possible," Everlasting said. "She is a queen!
No one, blade or cleverman or even madman, would
attack a queen. It is not in our nature."

"It has happened before," the Young Queen said.

"No." Everlasting shook his head hard. "You don't understand what it is to be a queen. She is the center of our hives, of our lives, our very reason for living. To be without a queen is to be lost utterly — if it were true that her sister killed my queen, still I would rather serve her than be queenless. Only the most perverse, the most unnatural — no. Wraith do not live without a queen."

"And yet," the Young Queen said. "That is not entirely true."

"Guide didn't have a queen when we met him," Sheppard said.

"Guide is one many of us would call perverse," Everlasting snapped, and Sheppard grinned.

"Ok, can't argue with you there."

"There is nothing wrong with Guide," the Young Queen said, "but Ronon could testify to the faults of a Wraith who called himself a king among your people. Or perhaps you approve of Runners?"

Everlasting glared at her. "We cull for food. We don't hunt for sport."

"My point exactly." The Young Queen smiled at him, and stiffly Everlasting bent his head.

"Even so — even admitting that this is possible — there is no proof."

"If we were to examine the bodies of the blades left by the nest, we might find proof," the Young Queen said, with a sharp look at Sheppard.

"They were fed upon," Everlasting began, and paused. "I see what you mean. They would have begun to heal, yes, but their clothes would still carry the marks of any wounds."

"We are not going back to the iratus nest," Sheppard said. "It's too dangerous."

"I must agree," Everlasting said. "Lacking a queen, they will swarm anything that approaches. And I do not think Salt can hold them a second time." Though if they could... He frowned, trying to remember what he had seen of the bodies. Had there been tears in the heavy coats? He had been focused on the shriveled features, the clear signs that they had — he assumed — given their lives for their queen. And perhaps they had, but — had there been other wounds? Had torn fabric moved in the faint breeze? He thought maybe it had, but he couldn't be sure. "If we grant that this is possible, and for argument's sake I do, what could he possibly hope to gain?"

"You would know that better than I," the Young Queen answered, and Everlasting had no response.

"I expect most of your queens have enemies," Sheppard said. "But the other thing is, if this is true, your queen's in danger."

"She's not my queen," Everlasting said, automatically. "But, yes, my queen has charged me with finding and protecting her. I will bear all this in mind, and will do what I can."

"You would be wise to do so," the Young Queen said, and there was a note in her voice that reminded him suddenly and sharply of Light Breaking. For an instant he wondered if there were some way she could understand their mental speech, as she seemed to understand them better than most — but he knew that was not pos-

sible. He managed not to bow as he would have done to
his own queen, and turned away.

Forge and Salt were still bent over their crude board,
drawn out now into a grid of nine, the counters sup-
plemented by dice to fill out the game. Everlasting
seated himself on the log behind them as though he
was watching the game, but his thoughts were elsewhere. If what the Lanteans said was true — and he
could see how it would fit, could see clearly how that
hypothesis explained more of what he had seen than
anything else they had thought of — then Moonwhite
was still in danger. He closed his eyes for an instant,
shutting out the firelight and the deepening night. If
Bell was the source of the infection, then all he would
have had to do was infect Moonwhite on her return
from the hive — or perhaps before? His breath caught
in sudden fear, but common sense reasserted itself. No,
if that had been the case, there would have been signs
of sickness before they left. Moonwhite was infected
on the homeward leg of her journey, and the strain
was virulent enough that they had to set down to feed.
And if it was that virulent, there was a chance it had
infected *Nimble*, and that might well explain the crash.
If the ship's systems were failing, it was no surprise
that the pilot could not put it down safely. So then
Bell persuaded them to seek the iratus nest? Why not
feed first? To preserve the treaty, perhaps — whether
or not Moonwhite agreed to it in the long run, neither
she nor Light Breaking wanted to make an enemy of
Alabaster unless they absolutely had to. And then at
the nest, something went wrong, and there was a fight.

Moonwhite was flung into the iratus nest — that might explain why she had sprawled so awkwardly, and why she had not yet awakened, if she had entered unprepared. Bell and the other blades fought, he fed on them to try to heal himself, but either he was attacked by the iratus or his wounds were too severe to heal immediately, and he collapsed where he was found. He had been healing then, he would have lived if he had been able to make it to the village to cull.

Dice you for your thoughts, Salt said quietly, his eyes hugely dark with the fire behind him.

Everlasting did not answer immediately, but rose to his feet and came to stand between the storymaker and the cleverman, resting a hand on each of their shoulders so that they could speak privately. *The Lanteans have proposed a solution,* he said quietly, and let the images spill over them, the story he had woven from the evidence and the Lanteans' suggestions unwinding like the clockwork in a child's toy. Salt hissed softly as he finished and he felt Forge take a deep breath.

Bell is a blade of Night. He could make the others choose the iratus nest over culling.

He couldn't force a queen, Everlasting said.

Not if they went mind to mind, Forge said. *But if she were ill, and he were subtle, offering suggestions with a little pressure behind them? It's possible.*

It was possible, Everlasting thought. Moonwhite would have been sick and afraid, and above all she clearly trusted Bell. *But why? What could he gain?*

The queen's death, clearly, Salt said. *But, more than that, he puts our two hives at each other's throats.*

To what end? Forge asked. *If we destroy each other, he's destroyed with us.*

Unless he serves another, Salt said.

There are no other queens who would agree to such a plan, Everlasting began, and shook his head. *At least, none that I know of or that we have contact with. I cannot see Alabaster doing this.*

There we're in agreement, Forge said, his tone wry. *What do we do now?*

Speak to Blaze, Everlasting began, but the words died as they were formed. If someone came to him with such a tale — no, he wouldn't believe it, not with more proof than they had to offer.

I have a thought, Salt said. *Let me tell a tale tonight. I will weave such a plot that Bell will betray himself, and that will be the proof we need.*

Dangerous, Everlasting thought. And if it goes wrong, we are no better off — but not so very much worse off, either. *Can you do it?*

I can, Salt said, and for the first time in years Everlasting was reminded that the storymaker was old and powerful, that he had served more than one queen in his day, and lived to return to his beloved Edge.

I'll hold you to that, he said, and lifted his hands from their shoulders. *And now — I must have at least some word with Blaze.*

Blaze came out from the queen's shelter to join him, shaking his head when Everlasting asked for news. *No change yet, though she has taken water.*

I will give her more, Bell offered, rising from where he had been sitting beside the entrance, and Everlasting stiffened. There was nothing he could do to stop him, and that was the best chance anyone had to harm Moonwhite. To his relief, Blaze shook his head.

Not just now. I've given her nearly a full container, let her absorb that first. Sit with her, though, while I speak with Everlasting.

And that, too, was undesirable, but could not be avoided. Everlasting moved away from the shelter toward the fire, and Blaze followed reluctantly. *Well?*

The Lanteans have made a suggestion, Everlasting said, *and I'm honor bound to put it to you.*

Blaze narrowed his eyes. *Why do I think I will dislike this?*

Because I don't much like it myself, Everlasting said, *but it matches the facts well enough that you must hear.* Carefully, he outlined Sheppard's theory, feeling Blaze withdraw from him as he spoke. *And you,* he finished, *can prove clearly that it is untrue, given that you know the man. He's a blade of Night, was he born to Moonwhite's hive?*

Blaze took a deep breath, tamping down an anger that burned like his name at the base of his thoughts. *He was born to Edge's hive long ago, and left before our queens were born. His hive was destroyed by Death, and Moonwhite was glad to welcome him. A more than competent blade, still spoken highly of among his age-mates.*

That is not the answer I was hoping to hear, Everlasting said at last, and Blaze gave a sour smile.

I expect it isn't. It's not the one I'd like to give you.

So it is possible, Everlasting said.

But unlikely. Blaze glanced over his shoulder toward

the shelter. *And you make me doubt whether I should leave him alone with her. Which could be the whole point.*

I don't want your queen dead or even harmed, Everlasting said. *I have made my choice, but yours is a worthy queen, and I am happy to see her hunt in company with mine.*

There is no proof, Blaze said. *And he is the only survivor here who is her man. The only person here who is her man besides me.*

Salt believes he can tell a tale that will cause him to betray himself.

Blaze's eyebrow ridges rose. *Do you believe it?*

I have seen him hold an entire hive in thrall, Everlasting answered. *And he was Edge's man. He has never chosen between her daughters.*

True. Blaze dipped his head.

I can't think of anything better, Everlasting said. *Let him try. And — one more thing? Tell Bell we plan to go in the morning to examine the bodies left at the iratus nest.*

Madness!

Everlasting nodded. *I won't do it, and Sheppard won't, either, but — if there is any truth to this, it should worry him considerably.*

Blaze nodded slowly. *I will do that much, yes. And I will watch my queen myself. But I do not believe this story. Only a Lantean would propose it.*

I wish that were so, Everlasting said, and turned away.

The darkness between the trees was impenetrable. On the Lantean side of the fire, the Marine Hernandez edged another branch into the flames, and the burning sticks above it collapsed, releasing a burst of sparks. Salt tilted his head to watch them spiral up toward the moonless sky, the stars obscured by a thin veil of clouds. It was a good night for story-making, with the darkness hugging close and the clouds to bring a breath of damp like the kiss of the hives' mists, as good a night as he could wish for, except for the stakes involved. He slanted a glance at the shelter where Moonwhite still slept, settled like a child in the bed of branches. He remembered her as a fruit-fed toddler, chasing her sister through the hive with shrieks of laughter, only to fall asleep in her sister's arms, curled together as though they had shared a single womb. They were the only surviving daughters of Edge, and he would not see either of them brought down, not like this.

That sparked a memory, a tale he had heard long ago, told by a rival to taunt him for being of the line of Night. It would serve, he thought, and rose slowly to his feet, exaggerating the stiffness of age. At his feet, he felt Forge tense, but Everlasting managed to look up with a fair assumption of idle curiosity. He could not see Blaze clearly, sitting with Moonwhite within the shelter, but Bell lifted his head as well.

"I have a proposition," Salt said aloud, pitching his voice so that the Lanteans could hear as well. "There will be no transport until morning, yes?"

There was a moment of silence, broken only by the crackling of the fire, and then Sheppard said, "Yeah, that's right."

"Then allow me to offer entertainment." Salt bowed

as he would to a consort, and saw the humans exchange nervous glances.

I would like a tale, Forge said, and there was a movement inside the queen's shelter as Blaze moved closer to the opening.

I see no harm in it, provided you do not disturb the queen.

I will not touch her mind, Salt promised.

Bell looked as though he wanted to protest, then shrugged, and settled back in his place.

"Ok, but how exactly is this going to work?" McKay asked, from the other side of the fire.

"I will shape an image so that all can see," Salt said. "An illusion only, and clearly such, but you will be able to see and hear as though you were yourself present."

He saw the humans exchange uneasy looks, and Everlasting said, "It would pass the time."

Sheppard bit his lip. "Ok," he said. "But just so you know, if anything attacks us, we're going to shoot it."

"And we will be in the line of fire, yes, I know," Everlasting snarled.

"That is not the sort of tale I had in mind," Salt said mildly. "In any case, you will know what is illusion and what is real."

"Ok, then." Sheppard nodded.

"Then let us begin." Salt reached into the pocket of his coat, found the little bag of aromatic resin that he always carried. He took a pinch of it and turned toward the fire, only to freeze at the sound of Ronon's weapon coming to life.

"Hold it," the Satedan said.

"What are you doing?" the Young Queen asked, almost in the same moment.

"It's an incense, from the resin of the daivo tree." Salt blinked, realizing what they must have thought. "It has no great physical effect, and none at all on humans. It merely helps me to focus, and that because I have trained myself to take it as such."

There was another silence, and then Ronon lowered his weapon. "Ok."

The Young Queen nodded as well, and Salt completed his gesture, tossing the pinch of resin into the flames. It ignited instantly, a brief puff of green-tinged flame and the familiar bittersweet scent, and he took a deep breath, focusing his will.

"Once before we slept, there were nine and ninety-nine, nine Mothers and their men." He let the familiar shapes dance across his thoughts, shaping them from fire and shadow, the faces of the nine Mothers flickering in the firelight. "And they are all worthy of a tale or nine or ninety-nine —" He let more images flicker past, familiar shapes that would remind the others of a dozen other stories, though what the Lanteans would make of them he did not know. "But this tale is of Night's lineage, of two of her daughters born at a single birth. For this was long ago, when still we hid from the Ancestors in the empty depths of space, and we had not yet learned everything we know today. So it was that Night conceived, but the egg split in her womb and formed two daughters, and she could not bear to choose between them, but instead bore both. They were called Dusk and Dawn, and were as like to each other as two eyes in one skull, each the mirror of the other."

So far, the tale was known, though not common: it had not been told often on Edge's hive because the daughters' endings were unhappy, and neither Light Breaking nor Moonwhite seemed inclined to request it, either. Still, it was familiar enough that he could draw on well-known images, shaping the story in the shadows beside the fire. The daughters reached adulthood, and became queens in their own right, each with their own hive. They did not dare hunt together, for fear of attracting the Ancestors' attention, and so with great regret they separated, each seeking out their own hunting grounds far from the Ancients and from each other. Once in a century, their paths might cross, and the sisters always greeted each other with fondness, and their men were allies and kinsmen. Each sister chose a consort, Dawn a blade of Cloud, whose thoughts were hot and sharp as the desert sands. But Dusk chose a blade of Night, cool and clever as a mountain stream as it leaps over boulders, and those choices were the first great difference between them in all their lives.

Salt took a breath, looking through and past his images to see the Lanteans watching from the far side of the fire. They looked alert and curious, the Young Queen frankly fascinated, while the others followed more carefully. Even Ronon seemed to be tracking the story, though neither he nor the Marines had put aside their weapons. As for his own people, they were neatly wound into the tale, relaxed in spite of themselves by the familiar forms. Now it was time to change the story.

"And so they went on, though neither sister had met the other's consort, until Sand, Dawn's Consort, encountered a ship of the Ancestors while culling for the hive, and as he fought to cover their retreat, his ship was destroyed under him, to Dawn's aching sorrow." He sketched the queen alone in her chamber at the heart of the hive, a bower empty of purpose without her chosen consort. "And at the same time, for the sisters' fates were closely bound together, Dusk's Consort, Rapid, took a party of his own to cull, and they, too, were attacked by the Ancestors. Only Rapid escaped through the Stargate, and he was so badly wounded that he fell unconscious on the very steps of the ring, unable to heal himself and too badly hurt to seek a place to feed.

"And that is where the blades of Dawn found him, lying beside the ring of the Ancestors, a stranger whom they did not know. So they brought him back to Dawn's hive and fed him and when he was conscious again, they brought him to the zenana for the queen to see. Weak as he was, Rapid looked into her eyes, and thought, this is the queen I want to serve. And so he told her he could remember nothing of his past, and because he was a blade of Night, and she did not distrust him, he concealed the truth and Dawn took him into her hive. And he was a blade of beauty and talent, and soon she took him into her zenana as well.

"But that was not enough for Rapid, who they called Stream. He had been a consort, after all, and he wanted to be a consort again. He wooed Dawn carefully, and it seemed as though she would claim him as her own. But before that could happen, word came that Dusk's hive was nearby. Dawn was delighted, eager to meet her sister, but Rapid was afraid, for once Dusk saw him, all his plans would come to nothing. And so he hatched a plan to keep the sisters from meeting, and to save his place, a man who seemed likely to be consort to two queens both living."

This is not how the story goes, Bell said, in spite of himself.

Salt did not pause, weaving image on image, shaping Dawn's bower again. *This is how I saw it on the hive of Queen Fireheart, a thousand years ago.*

He dishonors our queen, Bell said, to Blaze, who shook his head.

Go on.

Salt bowed. "So Rapid began to whisper among the blades of Dawn, saying that Dusk coveted her sister's hive and her sister's hunting grounds, which were safer than those of Dusk. And as he had hoped, the lords of the zenana came to Dawn and begged her not to trust her sister, but to postpone the meeting for a safer day. Even the hive's clevermen joined the plea. But Dawn refused them, saying she knew her sister and trusted her, and that all would be well. Her only concession was that she would leave the hive out of range, and meet Dusk at a world where they both culled, and that Dusk would do the same.

"Rapid knew he had only one chance left, and when Dawn went aboard the cruiser that would take her to the meeting, he went with her as consort-to-be. And as consort-to-be, he poisoned the ship, and forced it down on another world entirely. Dawn trusted him — how could she not, her chosen consort? And the other blades trusted him as well."

Salt could feel the tension rising, and shaped his images accordingly. Rapid had been a blade of Night, formed according to that canon, but now he gave the face a subtle push, making it more modern, so that it began to resemble Bell.

"And so he planned his final act: he would kill the others, for fear they might suspect, and he would cloud Dawn's mind so that she did not remember what he had done, or if he could not hold her thoughts, then he would kill her, too."

In his illusion, Rapid leaped to attack three other blades, who fell back, taken by surprise. They fought hard, but one by one Rapid overcame them, and stood panting over their bodies, his coat cut to ribbons and his skin ashen with hunger. Salt saw Bell snarl silently, but the blade mastered himself. It would only take one thing more, Salt thought, his hands trembling now with the strain of holding all the threads.

"But this," the Young Queen said, her voice clear and calm, "this — story — is very like what has happened here. Too like to be coincidence."

"I will let Bell answer that," Salt said, and Bell leaped for him, feeding hand extended. Salt ducked to the side, and tripped over one of the branches gathered for the fire. He fell in a heap, hunching his body to protect himself. Bell's hand caught his shoulder, claws tearing at the fabric of his coat. He felt the kiss of Bell's hand-mouth, the tug of life drawn from his body, and then Everlasting and Forge had wrestled him away. Salt tottered to his feet, aware of the Lanteans' weapons covering them from beyond the fire.

So, Blaze said, his own feeding hand flexing. *You admit your guilt.*

I do not! Bell glared at him, pinned between Everlasting and Forge. *He has insulted me — he accuses me of harming our queen! Of course I lost my temper. But this, this tale of his — there's no truth in it, none at all.*

But there is.

Salt's breath caught in his throat. Moonwhite emerged from the shelter, reaching out to take Blaze's arm to steady herself. She looked worn, and clearly needed to feed properly, but she was well and whole.

Clever Salt, she said. *You've guessed most of it. He has been holding me unconscious since we came to this camp.*

Blaze snarled at that, and made an abortive lunge in Bell's direction, but Moonwhite held him back.

"I don't want to intrude," Sheppard called, "but would you guys like to explain what's going on here?"

"I think there is much explaining to do," Salt said.

Forge shifted his grip on Bell's arm and shoulder so that he could set the claws of his feeding hand more firmly into Bell's skin. Bell snarled, but did not struggle: Forge had his hand planted solidly above Bell's spine, and Everlasting's feeding hand was pressed close to the blade's heart. Moonwhite leaned on Blaze's arm, her teeth bared in killing fury.

You, she said, eyes fixed on Bell. *You betrayed me.*

Forge heard the snap of the Lanteans' weapons, but did not dare look sideways to see them leveled. If they fired, Everlasting and Bell were both between him and the bullets, but he did not think they would be enough protection to spare his life.

"You want to tell us what's going on?" Sheppard called.

"Besides the obvious?" That was Salt, swaying from the attack and the broken story.

"It would be well if you spoke so that we all can hear," the Young Queen said.

Moonwhite did not look at her, gave no sign that she had heard, but spoke aloud, still staring at Bell. "I would have elevated to you to the zenana — would have allowed you to sire a son — and this is how you thank me! It was you who poisoned the ship, and you who infected us all, you who told me there was an iratus nest in the hills." Her eyes narrowed. "It was you who planned everything."

Blaze gave her a wary look. "Everything?"

"That is why you asked about Edge's zenana," Salt said, and sounded as though the words were startled from him.

"Just so." Moonwhite flexed her feeding hand. "As I said, I planned to allow him to sire a son — we had discussed it, both he and I, and I had also spoken to my Consort. There were anomalies when I calculated the genetics of our potential offspring — anomalies which Bell himself created. And thus I took him with me when I went to consult my sister, and left myself open to his treachery. To lift your hand against a queen!"

"You are not my queen." Bell flung himself forward, and Forge hauled him back, feeling blood against his palms as his claws bit deep. "You were never my queen."

"I took you in! I favored you." Moowhite snarled. "Worthless, faithless scum."

"My queen is Death," Bell answered. "And I will never serve another."

"Death is dead," Moonwhite said.

"If he's Death's man, he's planned this a long time," Forge said. "The blood fever — the Lanteans said it had been altered, but I could see no purpose in making it more virulent, except to kill. And that was always Death's way. She ruined everything she could not hold."

"Liar and fool." Bell lunged again, and Everlasting dragged him back, handmouth against his skin so that he froze, hissing furiously.

"Let me get this straight," Sheppard said. "This guy caused your ship to crash? And then — tried to kill you?"

Moonwhite gave him a long stare, as though she was seeing him clearly for the first time. "You are — the Consort of Atlantis?"

McKay made an odd sound that might have been laughter. The Young Queen said, "He is."

Moonwhite lifted her head, and Blaze said quickly, *We are in their debt. They brought us here, helped us to search.*

Why? Moonwhite did not take her eyes from the Young Queen. It was the look of a queen preparing to attack a rival, and Forge flinched.

I believe to preserve their alliance with Alabaster, Blaze said, and Moonwhite relaxed slightly.

Very well. She said aloud, "He sickened me and my men, and brought down our ship. While we were weakened, he clouded our minds — and that is on me, that I did not see it — and then told us of the iratus nest where I might be healed, since nothing he had done seemed to slow the fever. So we climbed up to the nest, and there, finally, his hand slipped, and I realized that he was pushing me to take this action. I broke his hold, and he and my loyal men fought —" Her face twisted, anger and grief. "While I was too weak to aid them. He beat them down, and flung me into the nest. The queen seized me, and I knew no more. Since he lives, I assume he fed on any survivors, the faithless coward."

"But it wasn't enough to heal him completely," Everlasting said. "We found him still unconscious, and you in the iratus queen's grasp."

"Death is dead," Moonwhite said again. "And you are mad."

"He is forsworn," Blaze said.

"And he has failed," Everlasting said. "Your queen lives, our alliance is unbroken, our friendship with Alabaster remains untarnished — we have met the Lanteans and found them to be true to their word, whatever other disagreements we have with them. Nothing he worked for has succeeded."

"Death is dead," Salt said. "And everything she worked for overthrown."

Bell twisted in their hands again. "She was the greatest queen of our day or any, and you are nothing but shadows. You have given us to the kine, and we shall fade to nothing."

"You will not be here to see it," Moonwhite said, with a grim smile. "He has tried to kill a queen, murdered his fellow blades, destroyed a ship of my following. Can anyone speak for him?"

"Not I," Everlasting said, and Forge echoed him. Salt shook his head in silence.

Blaze said, "There is none who can."

"So," Moonwhite said. "When you joined my hive, you placed your life in my hands. You pledged it to my service as a blade of Night and a man of my hive." She flexed her feeding hand. "I require that life of you."

And more honor than you deserve, Blaze said, *to die at her hand.*

You are a shadow of a true queen, Bell retorted, *and your turn will come.*

Moonwhite moved then, as quick as a striking snake, closing the distance between them in a single stride, her feeding hand fastening unerringly on Bell's chest. He cried out in spite of himself, his head falling back as the life was ripped from him. Moonwhite snarled and pressed closer, draining him in great gulps.

"Hey, you can't do that —" McKay began, and fell silent at the Young Queen's glare.

Under the queen's hand, Bell withered, his skin wrinkling, his hair thinning to nothing, his struggles fading. His eyes closed, and he fought to shape a snarl. *Fools.* It was the merest thread of thought, the last flicker of his life. *Death has a daughter.*

Moonwhite snarled again, but it was too late. Bell hung dead in Forge's grasp, and Forge released him with a gasp of fear.

That can't be true.

Everlasting let go as well, and the emptied husk slid to the ground at their feet. *He's still trying to breed dissension between our hives. Surely.*

Blaze shook his head. *Can we afford to believe that?*

Moonwhite stared at the body, breathing hard, her teeth still bared, blood on her claws and on her hand-mouth. *Fool he named me, and fool I am. I should not have killed him so quickly.*

He would not have said more than that, Salt said. *Everlasting is right, he sought to cause trouble to the very end.*

And you needed to feed, Blaze said.

Moonwhite shook her head. *This was not wisely done.*

But it is done, Salt said, *and we must face the consequences.* He tipped his head ever so slightly toward the Lanteans, standing with weapons ready. *All of them.*

Moonwhite shook back her hair and turned to face the humans. Forge took a step sideways, ready to place himself between the queen and the Lantean weapons. She was not his queen, he thought, but he owed her that much — owed his own queen to protect her sister. The two Marines looked shaken, and Ronon's lips were drawn back in a snarl that rivaled Moonwhite's. Sheppard looked uneasy, and McKay was shaking his head. Only the Young Queen stood impassive, her expression unreadable.

"Was that really necessary?" McKay said, plaintively. "I mean, really?"

"His life was forfeit when he raised his hand against me," Moonwhite answered.

A silence stretched between them broken only by the hiss and crackle of the fire. After a moment, Sheppard nodded reluctantly, and the Young Queen said, "We understand why you did it."

"Yes." Moonwhite hesitated then, and Blaze lifted his head in alarm.

Surely there's no need to tell them what he said —

Yes, Everlasting said, in almost the same moment, *I agree.*

Be silent. Moonwhite stared at the Young Queen for another handful of heartbeats and then abruptly her frozen stance eased. "There is a thing you should know, and before you say it, I am aware that I acted precipitously. With his last breath, he claimed Queen Death had a daughter."

Ronon said something under his breath that made the Marines exchange respectful glances, but the Young Queen gave a thoughtful nod, as though it did not surprise her.

"Oh, that's just great," McKay said, rolling his eyes. "That's just what we need."

"Is that possible?" Sheppard asked. "I mean — we'd have known if she was pregnant when she was killed, right? And if she'd had a kid before, wouldn't somebody have mentioned it?"

"If she had had a daughter born before she tried to bend us all to her will, I would have expected her to speak of it, yes," Moonwhite said. "It would have aided her cause. But if she conceived before the last battle, and placed the embryo in stasis in her hive — it's possible."

"Her hive was destroyed," the Young Queen said.

Moonwhite shrugged. "In another of her ships, then. That's not unknown. But I will agree it makes it less likely. And I will also agree that it is very possible that he lied. It would certainly suit him to leave us in fear."

Sheppard and the Young Queen exchanged looks, and Sheppard said, "So why are you telling us this?"

Moonwhite spread her hands. "You saved my life. I am in your debt that far, whatever comes of this agreement."

"Fair enough," Sheppard said.

And that, Forge thought, was proof enough that they would eventually agree to the treaty. They had worked with the Lanteans, and been treated with honor — more than that, had treated them as equals, and there was no stepping back from that line. In the meantime... He caught Everlasting's eye and together they dragged Bell's body into the woods away from the fire.

In the morning, the Lantean jumper arrived as promised, and delivered them to the field by the Stargate where their scout was waiting. Blaze delivered Light Breaking's people to their own waiting cruiser with promises of further contact soon, then set a course to rendezvous with Moonwhite's hive. Once the cruise was safely underway, he made his way aft to the quarters given over to the queen, hesitating for an instant outside the door before he felt the familiar touch of her mind.

Enter.

The door slid back at her word, and Blaze came in. This was not a zenana, or even proper queen's quarters; it was intended for a blade commanding, a single room with its bed inset into the curve of an inner wall that also hid the bathing chamber. Moonwhite was curled on a large armless chair, nestled comfortably in its thickly padded surface. She looked better than she had on the planet, though Blaze could feel her underlying hunger.

We are on course for home, he said. *We should be there in seven hours.*

Good. She shifted, gesturing with her off hand to indicate that he should take the space created, and Blaze perched carefully next to her. *It was well done,* she said, after a moment.

Blaze dipped his head. *Thank you. I feared —* And there he stopped, not wanting to admit all the things he'd suspected, everything that had crossed his mind since she had disappeared.

Moonwhite's smile was wry. *I know.*

Greatly daring, he let himself lean against her shoulder, and was rewarded by a small sigh of contentment. Mist rose from the floor, soothing skin dried by altitude and sunlight, and he closed his eyes, smelling the sweet-sharp scent of her hair.

We will have to accept this alliance, she said. *I always knew we could not fight the Lanteans. Now — now I doubt we could avoid their notice.*

I agree, Blaze said. He wouldn't like to go up against Atlantis's consort even in a fair fight; the Lanteans' technology negated the advantage the Wraith had always had, and their weapons might even tip the balance in the other direction. Better to make a deal than to risk open war.

Will Light Breaking agree?

My impression is that she was already leaning that way, Blaze answered. *I don't think this will change her mind.* He paused. *There is also the retrovirus to consider.*

Moonwhite curled her lip in a silent snarl. *Don't

remind me. Surely you see the problems as well as I.*

I do. But I am beginning to think there may be advantages as well.

Perhaps, Moonwhite said, and sighed. *Let's leave that for another day.*

Blaze bowed his head. *As you wish.*

She settled herself more comfortably against his side, her head on his shoulder, her fingers brushing his wrist. After so long apart, after all his fears, he was hyperaware of that touch, of her exhaustion and her hunger and her indomitable spirit. If she had been lost… He suppressed that thought, unwilling to look at it now that it was safely in the past, and felt her smile.

If I die, you should join Light Breaking.

I don't want to. He had spoken with more honesty than he had meant, and her fingers tightened, claws digging momentarily into his skin, silent reproof.

You will at least settle my people there.

Yes. He dipped his head again, grateful for so much grace, to be allowed to choose solitude however perverse that choice might be. *I will certainly do that.*

My sister will keep them safe. As safe as possible, in any case. You are, of course, free to do as you wish once that's done.

Thank you.

It was very peaceful sitting there, the mist drifting gently toward them, and Blaze let his eyes close again. Soon they would be back on the hive, but for now he could take this time simply to be with his queen, relax and bask in her presence.

When Bell held me unconscious, she said slowly, and

shook her head. *It was the oddest thing.*

Oh?

I dreamed I could feel another queen, sometimes close, sometimes far, but striving, I thought, to help me. To free me. And her touch, her presence — I would swear it was Steelflower.

Guide's queen who was killed? Blaze cocked his head to one side.

Moonwhite nodded. *Of course it couldn't have been her.*

I've heard tales, Blaze said. *Others have said they have felt her presence when they were in danger, helping and advising, just as some have said they have felt the Mothers.*

A tale for Salt, Moonwhite said, after a moment, and drew herself upright. *And there is work to do.*

Stay in touch...
Follow us on Twitter
@StargateNovels

Find us on Facebook at
facebook.com/StargateNovels

Sign up for our newsletter
at StargateNovels.com

THANKS!

STARGÅTE
SG·1.

STARGATE
ATLÅNTIS

Original novels based on the hit
TV shows **STARGATE SG-1** and
STARGATE ATLANTIS

Available as e-books from leading online
retailers

Paperback editions available from
Amazon and **IngramSpark**

If you liked this book, please tell your
friends and leave a review on a
bookstore website. Thanks!

CPSIA information can be obtained
at www.ICGtesting.com
Printed in the USA
LVHW041103180321
681839LV00025BA/78

9 781905 586745